C000015608

HEARTS UNDER FIRE

OPERATION: HOT SPOT

TRISH MCCALLAN

TRISH MCCALLAN INC.

ALSO BY TRISH MCCALLAN

Red-Hot SEALs Novels

Forged in Fire

Forged in Ash

Forged in Smoke

Forged in Ember

Operation: Hot Spot

Hearts Under Fire

Trust Under Fire

Loyalty Under Fire

Novellas

Spirit Woods

The characters and events portrayed in this book are fictitious. Any similarity to real persons, living or dead, is coincidental and not intended by the author.

This book was originally published as Bound by Seduction.

Text copyright © 2016 Trish McCallan

Cover Design: Frauke Spanuth, Croco Designs

Photographer: Wander Aguiar

Model: Brian

All rights reserved.

No part of this book may be reproduced, or stored in a retrieval system, or transmitted in any form or by any means, electronic, mechanical, photocopying, recording, or otherwise, without express written permission of the publisher.

Published by Trish McCallan Inc.

Printed in the United States of America

ABOUT HEARTS UNDER FIRE

Hearts Under Fire's timeline takes place several weeks prior to the events in Forged in Ash. Nor is it part of the four book story arc that spans Forged in Fire, Forged in Ash, Forged in Smoke and Forged in Ember. While Aiden's and Demi's storyline will continue in a full length romantic suspense novel, it will be a standalone romantic thriller and will not be part of the Fire story arc.

CHAPTER ONE

Demi Barnes paused in front of the tavern door to glare up. Her red sweater, red mini skirt and four-inch red stilettos turned an odd shade of fuchsia under the bright pink fluorescent light spilling down from the gaudy, blinking sign on the rooftop. Which kinda defeated the whole purpose of her fuck-me-now ensemble.

The *Mysteries of the Human Brain* documentary The Science Channel had aired earlier that week had linked the color *red* to male arousal. Not pink, not fuchsia—red.

With a sigh, she tugged down the leather mini-skirt and adjusted the plunging neckline of the figure-hugging sweater so it would leave *something* to her target's imagination. As she yanked the neckline up, her fingers tangled in the thin gold chain hanging from her neck.

A shaft of guilt struck. She should have taken the chain off—along with the diamond studded wedding band that dangled from it. But removing it felt wrong. She'd been wearing the diamond band, in one way or another, for seven years.

But then again, wearing the symbol of her everlasting love

for Donnie while she seduced another man felt wrong too... worse than wrong...it felt.... just...icky. So she carefully slipped the chain over her head and dropped it into the leather clutch that held her cell phone, driver's license, a small wad of cash and a sampling of condoms in every size and texture imaginable.

With one last tug on the mini-skirt and a final adjustment to her sweater, Demi squared her shoulders.

Last chance. There's still time to call off this hunting expedition, retreat home, and spend the weekend sucking down ice cream and watching movies.

But the thought of another night spent in front of the television was way too depressing. It was time to take charge of her life; rejoin the kingdom of the living. Donnie had been dead for three years now—three excruciatingly lonely years. He'd be the first to tell her to dust herself off and get back out there...connect with someone. Of course, he'd also insist that her current plan to alleviate her loneliness through sex was crazy...but she wasn't ready for a relationship yet. At least not a real relationship. Not one with the potential to develop into love.

What she was ready for, what she wanted with every tingle and twitch of her libido, was some good old-fashioned sex. Pure wicked sensation. A no-nonsense, no strings attached, no emotions allowed, sex buddy. And Aiden Winchester, the man who fit every one of her criteria, and tickled her awakening sexuality, was inside this bar—or so she'd been told. She just had to march through that door and find him...and seduce him.

Baby steps, Demi, baby steps...

As she reached for the door handle, the door swung open. She wobbled back on her skyscraper heels to give the brown haired, broad shouldered guy exiting the tavern some room. He scanned her, a quick up and down sweep that took in her spiky pink hair and red stilettos, as well as everything in between.

"Well, hello there," he said, stopping in his tracks. He

scanned her again, his pale blue eyes warming. "Are you looking for someone, or with someone?"

Looking for someone? As in, looking to hook up with some random guy?

Well, she was looking for a hookup, all right, but not with just anyone. Her libido had given her specific instructions on whom to bring home.

"I'm meeting someone here."

I hope...

Her voice emerged unwittingly breathless thanks to the sudden bounce of nerves in her belly. Not that her new admirer appeared to mind the Marilyn Monroe impression, judging by the way his blue eyes shimmered.

"Lucky someone," he murmured, his gaze dropping to the expanse of white skin and curves exposed by the plunging neckline.

Demi shifted uncomfortably, fighting the impulse to drag the neckline up. Which was ridiculous, considering she'd spent hours changing clothes in her quest to find the perfect combination of red, figure hugging clothes that would expose the most cleavage and thigh.

"Well..." Demi sidled toward the entrance to the tavern, or at least as close to a sidle as a girl could get in four-inch heels. "...see you around."

See you around?

Seriously Demi, your conversational skills have gotten so rusty they've sprouted holes and started leaking.

"Not so fast there, sweetheart," her admirer said, as he caught the edge of the door she'd started to open. "Most of the guys in there are fresh off rotation and haven't had a woman in months. You walk in there looking like that and you won't make it past the first table."

There was a grim edge to his voice.

Surely he was exaggerating.

From what she'd gathered from Kait, her best friend and resident Navy SEAL expert, the Bottoms Up Tavern was a favorite haunt for SEALs. Or at least the ones living near San Diego. And SEALs were some of the most self-disciplined men in the world. They had to be, to survive their profession...right? She'd be perfectly safe in there...wouldn't she?

Frowning, she stared down the plunging neckline of her sweater, which put everything she owned on display...and then there was the tight, red mini-skirt which barely covered her ass. She'd dressed to kill, or at least smother Aiden's reservations. But perhaps in her quest to punch through her target's reserve and spark a reaction she'd gone a mite too far?

"I'm sure I'll be fine. There must be other women in there," she said, shifting uncomfortably. He was standing so close she could smell the spicy musk of his cologne. Yet his closeness and scent did nothing to stir her fickle hormones, unlike Aiden, whose presence alone was enough to throw her body into a tingly, palm-sweating meltdown.

"Sure, there are women, but..." he trailed off and shook his head. "Sweetheart, no offense, but your guy's an idiot. He should never have let you walk into this place dressed like that."

"Excuse me? Let me?" Demi's voice rose indignantly.

He didn't back down. "Yeah—let you. He should know better. You clearly don't. No way in hell can I let you walk in there alone, so I'll play escort until we track down this guy of yours."

"That's hardly necessary," Demi stressed, as he opened the door and ushered her into a large, square room with wood tables and chairs full of tanned, muscled, hard-faced men.

She'd been right. There were women sitting at the tables too, quite a few of them, as a matter of fact. But most of them carried the brassy-haired, empty-eyed badge of someone who'd been around the block a time or twenty. And they'd all paired up with at least one guy, in some cases two, in others three and four.

Every eye in the room swung toward the door and locked on her. A good two dozen appreciative male gazes did the same up and down sweep of her red-clad figure as her self-appointed escort had done in the alcove. The women, however, didn't look nearly as happy to see her.

Several chairs scraped back.

Uh-oh.

"Relax," he murmured in her ear as he looped an arm around her shoulder. "I've got this."

From the way the previously avid eyes watching her suddenly lost interest and returned to their tables and conversations, the arm around the neck must be some kind of primitive signal.

"Let's find this guy of yours." That earlier grimness was back in his voice. He escorted her across the wood floor of the tavern. "You see him?"

Demi scanned the dozen or so tables scattered throughout the room. There were plenty of dark haired, lean bodied men sitting at those tables—but none of them were Aiden. A gleaming, mahogany bar ran the entire length of the left wall, but he wasn't among the men bellying up to the bar, either.

According to Kait, it was tradition for Aiden, as well as the rest of the men from his platoon, to celebrate their first night off rotation with a round of drinks at the Bottoms Up Tavern.

"I don't see him," she murmured, her stomach clenching and sinking simultaneously. She glanced at her escort. "This is the Bottoms Up Tavern, right?"

"It is." He glanced from table to table. "What's his name? I probably know him."

Yeaaaaaaah…nooooooo.

Her new admirer had the same lean, muscled frame and economical way of moving that Aiden had. Their eyes were the same too—oh, not the color, but the expression. Watchful, slightly suspicious. Like they were constantly on guard. There was no doubt in her mind this guy was a SEAL, and since Aiden's team hung out here, they probably did know each other.

If Aiden was here, in the restroom or something, then her escort would know his name soon enough. But if he wasn't here...the thought of everyone banging on Aiden's shoulders and teasing him about the pink-haired stalker who'd come looking for him...

She grimaced, the possibility rolling around in her belly like greasy, week-old sushi. Better to keep his name quiet so he wouldn't find out she'd been looking for him.

"Maybe he's in the restroom," she said, pretending not to hear his question.

He stared at her for one long moment, sharp intelligence glittering in his light blue eyes, before shrugging. "The john's in the back. There's a pool round and poker game back there too. Could be he's waiting for you there."

The tavern was oddly quiet as he escorted her along the bar toward the back room. The music was some light-rock, honky-tonk tune that had been dialed way back. So far back it barely vibrated against her eardrums or interfered with the conversations taking place around the tables. This had to be the quietest, most sedate bar she'd ever been in.

The back room was louder than the front had been, mostly from the shouts and curses erupting around the pool tables. Along the side wall a door stood open, a thick cloud of smoke clogging the doorjamb.

Demi scanned the men clustered around the pool tables.

Nope...

She checked out the poker table.

Nothing.

She shook her head at her escort's enquiring glance, aware that the pool and poker tables had fallen silent. She could almost feel the sexual buzz sweeping the room.

Her guardian muttered something beneath his breath.

"Excuse me?" Demi asked, trying to ignore the heated gazes tracking her every move.

"I said." He raised his voice and eyebrows. "That getup you're wearing should be classified as military-grade weaponry."

That coaxed a laugh from her. Too bad Aiden wasn't around to get a dose of her artillery.

"Any chance he's out with the smokers?" He nodded toward the smoke-filmed side door.

"He doesn't smoke." Demi sighed. "Maybe he's in the restroom?"

He studied her face thoughtfully, before turning to address a burly guy exiting the hall that led to the restrooms. "Hey Korfiafis, anyone in the john?"

The guy glanced in their direction, took one look at Demi and stopped in his tracks. He gave her one of those up and down sweeps that the guys in this place had perfected, only his ended with a leer. "Nah, it's all yours."

Demi could read the assumption on the guy's face. He thought they were headed to the bathroom to...to...she felt her face light up like a bonfire.

Her escort swung her around and headed back to the main room, away from all those intense, interested eyes. "He didn't know you were coming, did he?"

She swallowed hard and sent him a slightly sick smile. "Not exactly."

"And you couldn't pick up the phone? Let him know you were coming?"

Make sure he was going to be here?

Although he didn't ask it, Demi could feel the question hanging between them.

"It's...complicated."

Complicated, as in, it would be far too easy to say no over the phone, which wouldn't give her magical red outfit a chance to do its job.

A shadow crossed his face. He grimaced, and then gave her a one-armed shoulder squeeze. "Well there, Miss Complicated, let me buy you a drink?" When her stride faltered, he gave a wry laugh. "No strings. We'll just let the boys drool over you for a few minutes longer."

But rather than choosing a table in the middle of the room, where she'd be on display, he escorted her to a small private table against the back wall.

"Besides," he said, as he pulled out a chair for her, "could be your lucky bastard's just running late. This place starts hopping the closer it gets to midnight."

It wasn't until she sat down that Demi realized they had a perfect view of the tavern entrance. She'd see Aiden the moment he arrived...if he ever showed up.

After the waitress headed off to collect their drinks, her new friend leaned back in his chair and smiled at her. "So, you got a name?"

Demi squirmed. So far he'd been incredibly good natured about the babysitting detail he'd saddled himself with, but she knew nothing about him. For all she knew, he could be the biggest gossip on base. If she told him her name, how long before everyone on his team knew she'd showed up at the Bottoms Up Tavern looking to score? How long before Aiden found out? Or Kait?

Knowing Kait, she'd decide to play matchmaker.

Demi wasn't looking for a set-up—but boy, oh boy, were her hormones demanding some pulse pounding sex.

Aiden was perfect hook-up material. Just being in his general vicinity turned her insides to mush and her bones to jelly. Her body tingled and twitched and liquefied in all the right places. The sexual chemistry was off the charts, at least on her side of the equation.

But on his side?

She sighed in disgust. The man barely knew she existed, which was the entire purpose of her man-hunting attire. Everything from the red sweater with its plunging neckline to the stilettos had been handpicked to rattle his libido and catch his attention.

"So no on the name?" her protector asked wryly as the silence dragged on. When the waitress arrived with their drinks, he absently smiled his thanks. Lifting a hip, he pulled out a money clip, peeled off a single bill, and tossed it onto the drinks tray. "Guess I'll just have to make something up."

Demi smiled at that, and took a healthy sip of her wine and then another. Within seconds, a warm buzz washed through her, which reminded her she'd skipped dinner, and lunch...and she couldn't remember breakfast either. Possibly accepting this glass of wine had been a very bad idea.

But then, it looked like coming here had been a very bad idea. What had she been thinking? Well, other than catching Aiden's attention—finally—and enticing him into some hanky-panky. But that was the whole problem, wasn't it? She hadn't thought of anything past catching Aiden's attention. It hadn't even occurred to her he might not be here. Without her self-appointed escort as a buffer, she could have been in trouble by now—or if not in trouble, at least extremely uncomfortable.

She sighed and raised her wine glass to her savior. "Thank you."

He shrugged, looking uncomfortable, which made Demi smile. He really was cute, in a good-guy kind of way. Although he was of a similar height and build as Aiden, the resemblance ended there. Aiden's hair was black; so were his eyes, probably a carryover from his Arapaho ancestry.

Aiden was good-looking in an exotic, slightly dangerous, bad-boy kind of way. The kind of guy you hid from your mother and father. The tingling, stomach knitting, bone jarring, can't-catch-your-breath kind of way.

She'd been attracted to Aiden the moment she'd met him, even though she'd been happily married and completely committed to her husband at the time. But just because she loved Donnie with every cell in her body and every synapse in her brain, it didn't mean she hadn't noticed and appreciated Aiden's sexuality.

For a while, after Donnie's freak death, her attraction to Aiden had vanished beneath a landslide of grief and depression. She hadn't felt much of anything beyond pain and loss those first couple of years. But six months earlier, her sex drive had jolted awake.

One moment she'd been numb from the neck down, the next her body started reminding her through the most graphic, sweaty, sexual dreams that she was still alive, still young, still in her prime. And the man who unfailingly starred in those nightly porno escapades was Aiden Winchester.

While her handy dandy vibrator—which she was having to change the batteries on far too often—was alleviating the worst of the cravings, it couldn't compete with an actual man beside her in bed. There was just something super sexy about a hard, hot male body pressing her into the mattress. Something about the way men smelled and felt during and after sex that added to the replete satisfaction. She was tired of a proxy. She wanted the real deal beside her, on top of her, inside her.

She wanted Aiden.

But Aiden wasn't here.

Thoughtfully, she watched the front entrance open and several more men enter the tavern. Most of the guys in the tavern were hot in two specific ways—their lean, muscled frames and the economical way they had of moving. They carried themselves with the ease and grace of men at the peak of health and fitness. That alone was quite sexy.

If she let go of this obsession she'd acquired for Aiden, then any of the men in this place should satisfy her cravings, right? Take this patient, good-looking stranger across the table from her...if she stopped comparing him to Aiden, maybe he'd start tickling her hormones.

"I didn't catch your name," Demi blurted out, breaking the easy silence that had fallen between them.

His beer bottle paused in midair. Slowly, he set it back down again. "I thought names were off the table?"

Pursing her lips, she shrugged.

His blue gaze sharpened and dropped to her mouth and the crimson coating of sex-on-a-stick she applied to her lips just before heading into the tavern.

"I'd call you Pink, but I hear that's already taken," he said, his gaze finally breaking from her mouth to settle on her spiky pink hair. "Isn't red supposed to clash with pink?"

She laughed. The spiky pink hairdo had been her first rebellion against the depression and grief swallowing her whole.

"With the sweater and mini-skirt, I doubt anyone's even noticed the hair," she said wryly.

"And the shoes," he offered, lifting his beer bottle in a toast. "Nobody missed those shoes."

"Well." Demi fluttered her eyelashes at him. "They aren't called fuck-me-stilettos for nothing."

He choked on a swallow of beer and coughed hard a couple of times.

"How about we trade names," he finally managed, a cough still roughing his voice.

"All right," Demi said, leaning her elbows on the table and chin in her hand, which gave him the best view possible down her chest.

To her surprise, after one quick trip down the rabbit hole of her cleavage, he wrestled his gaze back to her face and kept it there.

"On the count of three?" He lifted his eyebrows.

Demi nodded, giving him an honest smile. She didn't have a clue why, but somehow his resistance to her heavy-handed flirting was oddly reassuring. Too bad he wasn't inspiring any palm-sweating or belly-fluttering, or any of the other signs her libido broadcast when it took an interest in someone.

"One. Two—" He started the countdown. "Brett Taggart."

"Demelda Rhoades."

Which wasn't a lie. Demelda *was* her given name, even though she never used it and Rhoades *had been* her maiden name.

"But everyone calls me Melda."

Which was the lie. Nobody called her Melda. *Thank God.*

"Demelda sounds like a fussy librarian," she added with a grimace.

He gave her one of those laser-eyed, up and down body scans. "Trust me, nobody's going to mistake you for a fussy librarian."

Oddly enough, rather than dropping to her cleavage, his gaze drifted to her hair as he made the pronouncement.

Demi took another sip of wine, relaxing as a wave of warmth rolled through her. It didn't have the tingling in all the right places of sexual heat; more like the thick internal glow of an alcoholic haze, which was such a shame, because she really wanted to be attracted to this guy.

Hoping the alcohol might awaken her libido, she drained her wine glass.

He studied her face, a sharp intensity in his eyes before frowning.

Why? Could he tell the single glass of wine was giving her a generous buzz thanks to her lack of dinner, lunch and breakfast? Was he the kind of man whose code of honor forbade him from taking a woman home if he thought she was incapacitated?

Donnie had been that kind of man.

A shaft of grief and longing struck. Her fingers tightened around the wine glass until they turned white. After a couple of deep breaths she cast the pain aside. Tonight was about launching a new life, taking those first baby steps to stave off the loneliness—she couldn't allow memories of happier times to derail her.

"You okay?" His voice was very quiet, his blue eyes gentle and understanding.

Oh yeah, this guy—Brett, wasn't it?—this Brett was excellent at reading people. He'd instinctively picked up on her pain. He'd probably be great in bed, too, knowing what a woman wanted before she knew it herself. He really was the perfect test subject. Now if she could just rustle up a kernel of sexual interest in him. Maybe she just needed some physical stimulation to awaken her libido.

She ignored the little voice in the back of her head reminding her that she'd never gotten physical with Aiden, yet the sexual charge was off the charts.

"Would you like to take me home?" she blurted the question out with absolutely no finesse and cringed at the gaucheness. Not that her escort seemed to mind the boldness.

"Every guy in this joint wants to take you home," he said, after an awkward pause.

Score one for brain science. Her red camouflage had worked

like a charm. She just wished the knowledge wasn't quite so anticlimactic.

She worked to infuse some enthusiasm into her voice. "Great! So how about we blow this joint?"

A frown knit his brow and he cocked his head slightly. "You sure that's what you want?"

There was something in his eyes she couldn't quite place, and he hadn't exactly jumped at her offer. Of course, he knew she'd been looking for someone else. Maybe he didn't like being second best.

"You're not like leftovers, if that's what you're thinking," she said.

He smiled slightly and shook his head. "Not an issue. Trust me, in bed you won't be thinking about anyone but me." It wasn't empty arrogance, either, more like pure confidence. But then a shadow slipped through his eyes. "You just seem... conflicted. You sure this is what you want?"

Conflicted...

Well, that sounded better than uninterested.

"I'm sure," she assured him stoutly, although sudden doubt had chilled her arms and legs.

"Okay." Brett pushed his chair back and rose to his feet.

The scrape of their chair legs grating against the wood floor echoed in Demi's ears as she followed him up. Her palms picked up a greasy film and her stomach rolled. Okay, maybe she wasn't quite so sure after all.

This time the arm he slipped around her waist felt like a strait jacket. By the time they stepped through the tavern door, and into the humid San Diego night, her cold feet had stiffened her entire body.

"Relax," he said with wry amusement. "I'm just taking you home."

Possibly he'd picked up on her misgivings through the sudden rigidity that had infected her muscles.

She gulped down a deep breath of the thick, floral scented air and sighed. "I'm sorry. I guess I wasn't as ready as I thought."

"You're allowed second thoughts. Thirds and fourths, even," he said, dropping his arm from her waist.

"You don't need to take me home. I'm perfectly capable of driving. Besides, I live in Coronado."

"Sweetheart, you're unsteady as hell. It's either a cab or my truck. Just keep in mind that if you choose a cab, we could be waiting here forever. If you choose my truck, I'll have you home lickety split."

She paused. "I'm not used to these shoes."

Which was true, but a good share of the unsteadiness he'd commented on came from the wine on an empty stomach. He was right. It wasn't safe for her to drive. But was it any safer to crawl into a stranger's truck? Other than his name, she knew nothing about this guy, and she could hardly call Aiden or Kait for his report card, not if she wanted to keep this night's folly to herself.

But the thought of waiting in the parking lot while a steady stream of leering men passed by on their way in and out of the tavern...she shuddered.

"Tell you what, to ease your mind about climbing in the rig with me, why don't you call a friend, give them my name and the truck's plate number."

There he went again, reading her mind and the suggestion did have merit—*if* she had someone she could call. Unfortunately, over the last three years she'd lost touch with all her friends except for Kait.

But he didn't need to know that, did he? All business, she opened her clutch and grabbed her cell phone, picked a number at random, and texted his name along with the plate number of the huge black truck he stopped in front of. She pretended to hit send, before dropping the phone back into her purse.

"You all set?" he asked, holding the passenger door open for her.

She nodded and hoisted herself inside, feeling her barely there skirt slide indecently high up her thighs. Lifting her butt, she tugged it back down before securing her seatbelt. As Brett shut the passenger door and walked around the hood to the driver's side, she stared at her Volkswagen Beetle. She'd have to collect it in the morning.

"So where we headed?" he asked as they pulled out of the parking lot.

Demi rattled off her address and driving directions, and sat in silence as he navigated out to the freeway. With each rotation of the truck's wheels, the sense of letdown sank a bit deeper. This wasn't how she'd pictured the evening ending, or with whom she'd be ending it.

Half an hour later they pulled up in front of her condo building and he cut the engine. Turning to face her, he offered a slow smile. "Well, you livened up my night, I'll give you that."

On impulse, she leaned over and pressed her lips against his, then held her breath...hoping.

His mouth was soft and warm against hers, but...nothing.

No tingles, no sparks, no chills.

His arms lifted, slipping around her waist.

Man, she was being so unfair. From the way his arms were contracting and drawing her closer, the kiss had stirred something in him, something she had no intention of appeasing. Unable to face what might be lurking in his eyes, she ripped herself out of his arms, scrambled out of the truck and bolted for the entrance to her condo building.

It wasn't until she was in the elevator, on her way up to the fifth floor, that she realized she'd forgotten her clutch in his truck.

CHAPTER TWO

His hair still wet from the shower, Aiden Winchester opened his bedroom door and followed the scent of freshly brewed coffee and frying bacon. The condo lay quiet around him as he made his way down the hall. Both his roommates'—Tag's and Trammel's—doors were closed, but the smell of food was a clear indication that Trammel at least, their resident cook, was up.

He tracked Trammel to the stove, where he was standing with a spatula at the ready, staring intently at a skillet packed with fluffy, sunny-side-up eggs. As Aiden helped himself to some coffee, he glanced at the paper towel-shrouded platter with its mountainous cargo of bacon.

"You expecting the whole team?" he asked around a jaw-cracking yawn.

Trammel shrugged. Dragging a skillet of hash browns off the back burner, he expertly flipped them. "You get your run in?"

Aiden simply nodded. He'd traded an extra hour of slumber for a long, quiet jog through the streets of San Diego while the city slowly came awake around him. It wasn't like he'd been getting any sleep anyway—at least, not of the restful variety—

not with Demi climbing into his dreams and taunting him with her bare, silken skin.

He glanced at the stove's clock, urgency buzzing through him. He'd hoped the long, slow jog would curb the edgy tension, but it was getting harder these days to control his hunger. He'd waited a long time to stake his claim—too damn long. The reasons behind the endless wait had been sound, but that hadn't made the intervening years any less frustrating.

It was time to make a move.

He would have done it last night, if not for the damn bachelor's party, an invitation impossible to reject, since he was the best man.

He glanced at the clock again and grimaced. At barely six-thirty in the morning, it was too damn early to show up at her door. He needed to kill at least another three hours, which gave him plenty of time for breakfast.

"Tag up?" Aiden asked around another yawn.

"Not yet." Trammel took a couple steps to the right and opened a cupboard dragging down a stack of mismatched plates. "Looks like he has company."

"Company?" Aiden's coffee cup paused on its way to his mouth. "He's got a woman in there?"

"Looks like it." Trammel's lip quirked. "Assuming he hasn't taken to carrying a purse." At the lift of Aiden's eyebrows, he laughed. "There's a black purse sitting on the mail table," he said, referring to the waist-high wood table just past the entry where everyone dropped their keys, mail, weapons, or anything else they happened to be carrying when they walked through the door. "Didn't you notice it?"

Aiden shrugged. While a purse should have stood out in a house full of men, he'd had other things on his mind.

"Well, that's a first," Aiden said, around another yawn.

Tag hadn't even brought Sarah to the condo before the big split, but then he and Trammel hadn't exactly hidden their disapproval of that relationship either. What the hell had Tag been thinking, anyway? You didn't poach a teammate's girl, and Sarah had been *engaged* to Mitch, for fuck's sake. She'd been off limits.

Still, Tag hadn't looked at another woman since she'd gone back to Mitch. And last night would have been a tough one if he still had feelings for her. A reminder her wedding was right around the corner. Maybe he'd taken another woman into his bed in the hopes of driving Sarah from his mind.

As Trammel filled two plates with eggs, hash browns and a pile of bacon a rat-tat-tat sounded on the front door.

"Mooch." Aiden instantly recognized their teammate's signature calling card. "How the hell does he do it?"

Somehow the damn man always managed to show up when food was about to hit the table. He was particularly clever about showing up after the pizza delivery guy had been paid and sent on his way.

While Trammel let Mooch in, Aiden filled up a third plate with eggs, hash browns and bacon. If they let Mooch fill up his own plate, there wouldn't be anything left for Tag and his new lady.

"Hey," Mooch said as he walked into the kitchen. "Either of you get a look at Tag's new piece of tail?"

Aiden handed Mooch his plate and rummaged in the silverware drawer for a couple of forks. "Not yet. You?"

Mooch shook his shaggy blond head, absently accepting the fork Aiden handed him. "They were gone by the time I hit the BU last night. Been hearing about her all night, though. Squirrel says she's grade one dyn-o-mite. Dressed to score, with spiky pink hair."

Spiky pink hair...

A heart-shaped face with a stubborn chin, brown—slightly tilted—eyes, and a prickly mess of spiky pink hair burst into Aiden's mind. The bright pink hairdo had given him pause the first time he'd caught sight of it, mostly because he'd been dying to dig his fingers into the cloud of soft brown hair that had floated around her shoulders prior to the new hairdo. But not even the neon blast of color and texture riding the top of her head had smothered his craving for her.

It had been three years since her husband's death. Three endless years. He was done with waiting. It was time to step up and remind Demi that she hadn't followed her first love into the grave.

He carried his plate into the living room and settled on the couch, resting his feet on the coffee table. As he worked through the food, he strategized the coming siege. Although ST7 was fresh off rotation, that didn't mean much these days. With the world in a constant state of unrest, and new terrorist cells trying to make a name for themselves every day, his team could be called into action at any moment. He needed to make sure Demi was bound to him permanently by the time he was dragged away again. He needed to make sure she was as obsessed with him as he was with her. It was the only way to make sure she'd still be single and available when he returned from the next rotation.

He'd just scooped up the last bite of egg topped hash browns when he heard the front door open. Since Trammel was sitting in the recliner across from him, Tag must have been outside. Jogging, most likely; the man ran as often as Aiden did, and probably for the same reason. To make sure his body was too damn tired to react to memories of a woman.

Sure enough, when Tag stepped into the room his t-shirt

was soaked with sweat. So was the waistband of his sweatpants. The guy had been going at it hard, for a long time, but from the tension carving his face it hadn't helped a damn bit. Apparently, neither had the gal he'd brought home the night before.

Aiden could sympathize. Almost. Tag should have never gone after Sarah in the first place, not with Mitch in the picture. He'd avoided the hell out of Demi when she'd been married, and her husband hadn't even been a teammate.

"Bro." Mooch dropped his polished plate onto the coffee table and leaned back against the couch cushions with his fingers laced behind his head, watching Tag disappear into the kitchen. "You're supposed to spend that energy on that sweet little thing you picked up last night, not on pounding the pavement all by your lonesome."

"You heard about that?" Tag asked, reappearing in the kitchen doorway with a piece of bacon in hand.

"You picked her up at the BU. Everyone heard about it," Mooch said absently. His eyes locked on the table next to the entryway and he rose to his feet. "Well now, what do we have here?"

Aiden had to admit the shiny black rectangle of leather looked odd sitting there next to the sets of keys, boxes of ammo, and the guns.

Tag followed Mooch's gaze. "She left it in my truck when I dropped her off last night. Guess I'll pay her a visit later today."

"Ah, the classic move a woman makes when she wants an excuse for the post-fuck meet up," Mooch drawled, his voice brittle with cynicism. "Don't fall for it, bro. Mail the damn thing back to her." But a few seconds later the cynical tone shifted to admiring. "Hey, this is a sweet piece."

The reverence in the statement brought Aiden's head up. There was no way in hell the man was talking about a purse. He grinned on finding a sleek, black beauty of a gun in his team-mate's hand. A shiny, compact, unidentified pistol.

He exchanged intrigued glances with Trammel and they rose to their feet in unison, converging on the table. He recognized the weapon on closer examination, even though he'd only seen it on Smith and Wesson's and Shooting Illustrated's websites.

"Hell, you picked up the *Shield?*" he asked, moving in for a closer look. "The .40 caliber?"

At Tag's nod, he turned back to study the pistol in Mooch's hands. While the *Shield* had released over a year earlier, they'd been on rotation at the time. But the early reviews had been stellar. It had been heralded as the first compact, single stack, conceal carry weapon that retained the ergonomics and handling capacity of the original Smith and Wesson M&P. He'd been dying to get his hands on one since reading that first review.

"Picked her up yesterday," Tag said, polishing off the first piece of bacon. "She's a real sweetheart too. Sent two boxes of ammo through her yesterday, and not one malfunction."

"How much you pay for her?" Aiden accepted the gun Mooch passed to him. He hefted it, checking the balance. It felt perfect in his hand—fit his grip as though it had been made for him alone. Comfortable as a veteran pair of combat boots.

"Four and a half. I'm heading to the range after I clean up. You're welcome to put her through her paces." Tag's gaze skipped between the three of them clustered around the weapon.

Aiden passed the gun on to Trammel and glanced at the DVR. The red letters glowing on the machine claimed it was barely past seven. Even adding on the half hour it would take to get to her condo complex, it was still too early to start hammering on her door.

"When you heading to the club?" Aiden asked. If he demanded the first set of targets, he'd have plenty of time to get a little practice in, and make a quick trip to Rocky's House of Guns to pick up one of these babies for himself, before heading over to Demi's place.

"An hour?" Tag disappeared into the kitchen and returned with several more pieces of bacon. "I need to shower first and drop off the purse."

"An hour?" Mooch repeated with a halfhearted leer as Aiden handed the pistol to Trammel. "That's all you're giving her for an encore?"

Ignoring Mooch's comment, Tag polished off the last of his bacon as he headed down the hall toward his bedroom.

Trammel set the *Shield* back down on the table, thumped Aiden on the shoulder, and dug in his pocket, emerging with his keys. "I'm gonna head to the range now. Get some solid shooting in before we start playing with Tag's new baby."

Mooch waited until the front door had clicked behind Trammel and Tag was out of sight before shooting Aiden a wicked grin. "Squirrel said Tag's score was hotter than a land to air lock."

Aiden ignored the comment as he collected the plates. He'd just deposited them in the sink when Mooch let loose with a long, low wolf whistle.

"Holy Hell." Mooch whistled again. "This gal came packing."

Aiden turned to find Mooch standing just outside the kitchen entry, peering into her open purse.

"You ever heard of privacy?" Aiden asked in disgust. But then Mooch's comment caught his attention. *Packing?* "She carrying concealed?"

Mooch laughed. "Only if you consider condoms a deadly weapon."

Intrigued, Aidan headed over. "No shit. She's carrying condoms?"

"A whole damn party pack." Mooch pulled out a driver's license and studied it intensely. "That spiky pink hair is hotter than Kubal Ms. Demelda Barnes."

Aiden stopped cold on his way across the kitchen. Demi's last name was Barnes and her hair was pink and spiky.

A coincidence. Just a coincidence.

But unease unfurled inside him. That was one hell of a coincidence. Demi could even be short for Demelda.

"Let's see where you live, Ms. Demelda." Mooch lifted and tilted the license, then shot Aidan a smirk. "2631 Westbury Drive. Now that's an address I need to familiarize myself with."

2631 Westbury.

The address blew through Aiden's mind like a winter storm front. Kait, his sister, lived at 2631 Westbury Drive, condo 607. And Demi lived one floor down—condo 512. He knew that with absolute certainty, because he'd paid for the place. Not that Demi realized that, or would ever realize that. Hell, Kait didn't even know.

He wasn't aware of moving, but somehow he was standing beside Mooch.

His hand was so tense it ached, as he reached for the small rectangle of plastic. With his breath frozen in his chest, Aiden forced himself to glance down. Recognition slammed into him with the driving force of an AK-47 fired at close range. His chest went icy hot and then numb.

He smoothed his twitching thumb over the miniature glossy photograph—high cheek bones, a sharp chin attached to a heart shaped face, dark, grieving eyes beneath spikes of neon pink hair.

Demi...

His Demi...

Had been Tag's fuck the night before.

"I should be the one to return the purse..."

Mooch's voice echoed with predatory intensity in Aiden's ears.

"Break in a couple of those condoms...give her a taste of a real man."

One moment Aiden was just standing there, his hand clenched around the driver's license with such force one of the plastic edges had cut into the crease at the base of his thumb, spawning a thin, trickle of blood. The next moment he'd grabbed Mooch's arm and jerked him around, and his clenched fist was headed for his teammate's mouth.

Aiden's knuckles connected with Mooch's jaw with the force of a cannonball. The impact snapped his teammate's head back and sent him staggering into a wooden table which splintered beneath his weight. Already off balance, Mooch hit the floor with a crash. What was left of the table disintegrated beneath his weight. The purse plopped to the ground beside him.

A wave of sheer pain ricocheted up Aiden's arm and exploded into his elbow, setting off a burst of hellacious tingling. Shaking his arm and breathing hard, Aiden took a shaky step back. A vicious ache sprang up, migrating between his head and heart.

Lying there at Aiden's feet in stunned silence, Mooch worked his jaw a time or two, before slowly climbing to his feet.

"What the fuck, bro?" His gaze watchful Mooch used his thumb to wipe a trickle of blood from his mouth and took a cautious step back.

Aiden's teeth were gritted so hard he couldn't draw breath, let alone talk.

Tag charged down the hall. Naked, dripping hair plastered to his head, and rivulets of water running down his chest and thighs, he skidded to a stop behind the couch. His Glock extended in a two handed grip, he swept the living room.

By God, the asshole hadn't managed to grab a towel, but he'd found the time to weapon up. Typical.

When nothing dangerous presented itself, Tag lowered the Glock. He studied the splintered table, then raised his gaze to Mooch's bloody, swelling lip. "What happened?"

Mooch's intense gaze never left Aiden's face. "Your room-mate's gone schizoid."

"Aiden?" Tag's voice rose. He shook his head, disbelief stamped across his face. But when he turned his attention to Aiden, whatever he saw brought a cautious frown. He shot Mooch an accusing glance. "What did you say to him?"

"Nothing, bro, he just went off on me."

Absolutely still, Aiden fought to wrestle the rage back. It was a damn good thing his weapons were stored in the gun safe and that Tag's new toy was under the table rubble, because the impulse was strong to take up target practice on the parts of Tag's anatomy that should have been covered by a towel.

"Aiden?" Tag prompted. At Aiden's silence, he dropped his gaze to the floor and scanned the wreckage. His focus quickly locked on the black purse, with the pool of condoms and cash surrounding it. His eyebrows snapping together he turned to scowl at Mooch. "You rooted through her purse, you asshole?"

"Fuck you," Mooch snapped back, swiping again at the blood trickling down his chin. "I just wanted to see what she looked like."

"See what..." Tag checked out the purse again, before back-tracking to Aiden. His gaze sharpened when it reached Aiden's clenched fists. "What you got there, bro?"

Battling the urge to converge on Tag and start swinging, Aiden glanced down. A sharp, reddish edge of plastic poked through the space between his thumb and forefinger.

Demi's license.

He opened his fist. When the plastic rectangle didn't budge, he shook his hand and watched it break loose and fall to the floor.

Tag stared at the tiny image with its blast of pink hair and realization settled over his face. He glanced at Mooch. "You better go."

"I ain't leaving you alone with him."

"He didn't hit *me*," Tag pointed out dryly.

Cold amusement curved Aiden's lips. He wanted to hit Tag. Every muscle in his body tightened beneath that impulse. Christ, the thought of Tag touching her, covering her—he shuddered, his fists clenching.

"Go," Tag said, his voice clipped. While the command was directed at Mooch, his wary gaze never left Aiden's face.

Mooch finally shrugged. Turning, he headed for the door. Tense silence stretched between Tag and Aiden as they listened to Mooch's boots ring out against the tile.

Tag waited until the door opened and closed. "You know her."

Aiden opened his mouth, but could only manage a low growl. Jesus Christ, he sounded like an animal.

"Just so we're clear," Tag said in a slow, clear voice. "I didn't go looking for her. She was the one looking, and I never—"

With a feral snarl, red mist clouding his mind, Aiden stalked forward.

Tag drove a halfhearted fist into Aiden's belly to back him up. "God damn it, stand down and listen to me. I took her home, and we kissed, but—"

Aiden swung, aiming for the bastard's mouth. The asshole wouldn't be kissing anyone for a very long time. He'd make sure of it.

Tag blocked the blow with his elbow, and sent another fist

into Aiden's abdomen. "Son of a bitch, *listen to me, you crazy motherfucker.*"

Aiden swung again, and while Tag was busy deflecting that blow he leaned in for a sharp knee to the groin, hoping to neuter the bastard.

With a strangled hiss, Tag folded, his hands instinctively dropping and cupping to protect his genitals. "God damn it," he bellowed, still hunched over. "I didn't touch her, okay? I didn't fucking touch her."

Breathing hard, that red mist hissing through his mind, Aiden backed up. The beast inside him demanded action, retribution, revenge, so he struck where he knew it would hurt the worst.

"Like you didn't touch Sarah?" he snarled. "What is it with you and poaching teammate's girls?"

"You don't know a fucking thing about that," Tag shot back. He straightened, fire crackling in his eyes. "And you should be kissing my ass. The way she was dressed, every guy in the joint was panting after her. She sure as hell didn't act like she was *your* girl."

"She's off limits," Aiden roared, his voice bouncing off the walls. He stepped forward again, his fists clenched.

Tag squared off against him, his fists rising as well. "Maybe you should tell her that? Or better yet, how about trying your luck with her instead of cockblocking when someone else goes after her?"

Aiden's muscles tightened to the point of pain. "Maybe you should work on getting your own love life online instead of using Demi as a substitute for Sarah."

Tag went rigid, his face paled. "Leave Sarah out of it."

Aiden smiled and drove for the kill. "Oh, I think Sarah took herself out of it when she chose Mitch over you. How does it feel knowing she's waking up next to him right now, that they're probably getting it—?"

He stumbled back several steps beneath a series of vicious blows to his abdomen. Before he had a chance to recover, a right hook came out of nowhere, snapping his head back. Pain exploded in his jaw, but it was quickly followed by a tingling numbness. With a silent snarl, he launched himself forward, only to find himself jerked back. The sound of cloth ripping sounded behind him and his shirt slipped off his right shoulder.

"What the God damn fuck! I told Mooch he was crazy when he called." Trammel's voice cut through the thick air like a bull horn. "Stand down, both of you." He grabbed Aiden's arm, jerking him back, then stepped in front of him to shove Tag back as well. "What's wrong with you two? This kind of crap is exactly why there's a code. You remember the code," he snapped, disgust thickening his voice. "Bros before—" He broke off to shove Tag back again, even harder. "God damn it, don't even think about it, I'll lay you out good."

Which was enough of a threat to force Aiden back too. While Aiden's exercise of choice was jogging, Trammel's was boxing. The guy had a right and left hook that could knock you flat for a week. As he stepped back, he heard something crunch beneath his boot. Easing to the side he discovered a squished tube of lipstick. Next to it, Demi smiled up at him from the small plastic rectangle.

He stooped to pick up her driver's license, but his swollen fingers wouldn't bend with enough dexterity to grasp the damn thing. He grabbed her purse instead and opened it wide, but before he had a chance to sweep everything inside, a brilliant glitter caught his eye. Using his throbbing forefinger, he separated a diamond ring from the wad of cash it had been partially hidden within.

Her wedding band.

For one long moment he crouched there, staring at the glittering object. Fourteen months ago, the last time he'd seen her, she'd still been wearing the ring on her middle finger. Yet here it was now, threaded through a thin gold chain. He wasn't sure why the discovery of her wedding band in her purse felt like another blow to his chest. Maybe because he'd wanted to be the reason the band came off her finger, or maybe it was something much simpler—like the urgent questions the discovery raised. How long had the ring been off her finger? How often was she hiding it away while she hit the bars?

And most important of all, just how many guys had she picked up in the past year?

It took a few moments for his muscles to unlock and allow movement so he could sweep her belongings back into her purse, and a few more seconds to find his keys in the rubble. When he finally straightened, Trammel was still playing the buffer, a hand out-stretched toward Tag, like he was a damn street cop.

Tag didn't look like he was any more willing to drop the fight than Aiden was. He raised his eyebrows, pure disgust crossing his face, when he caught sight of the purse in Aiden's hand.

"Oh yeah, that's brilliant, dude," he said, his face twisting into a sneer. "Nothing like having it out with her when you're all amped up and look like shit."

Aiden gritted his teeth, wishing he could claim that he hadn't been headed over to Demi's place, but yeah—that was exactly where he'd been going. Forcing himself to turn away, he stalked toward the front door. He sure as hell couldn't stay here.

"Damn it, Aiden, hold up," Trammel said from behind him.

Aiden kept walking. When he reached the front entrance, a hand closed over his shoulder. Fists lifting, he pivoted, watching as Trammel jumped back with his hands in the air.

"I swear to God," Trammel snapped, irritation glittering in his dark eyes. "I've had it. You swing at me, and I *will* drop you. We clear?" He waited for Aiden's tight nod. "Good. And Tag's not wrong. You're a God damn mess. At least clean up the blood, put an ice pack on that lip, and change shirts."

The moment the words blood and lip hit the air, his mouth started throbbing. So did his jaw. A trickle crawled down the side of his mouth. Since he couldn't get his fingers to uncurl, he swiped at it with the back of his hand and stared at the smear of blood sprawled across his wrist. Trammel was right. He did need to clean up. But Jesus, if he ran into Tag inside...with the anger still churning at high boil on both sides...yeah, the condo might not survive another round between them. He'd be smarter to head to Kait's place, take a shower there, and wait for his blood pressure to fall before hunting down Demi.

He glanced down. His jeans weren't in bad shape, just a spot or two of blood. His face and shirt had borne the brunt of the abuse. So after a long, hot shower, all he'd need was a fresh shirt.

Lifting his head, he studied Trammel thoughtfully. They were around the same size, and the shirt Trammel was currently wearing looked clean enough.

"You want to make yourself useful?" Aiden asked, lifting his arm and wiggling his stiff, aching fingers. "Give me your shirt."

"Oh, for Christ's sake." Trammel tilted his head back and stared at the ceiling, his mouth moving like he was silently counting to ten.

"Trust me," Aiden said grimly. "You don't want me walking back in that room. Not if that bastard's still in there."

Swearing, Trammel dragged his shirt over his head, balled it up, and fired it at Aiden's head. "I hope to God you're not headed off to see this girl, because Tag's right about that too," he said, watching Aiden snatch the shirt out of the air. "It's a bad idea. You confront her in your current mood and she'll never talk to you again."

Aiden clenched his jaw, another wave of anger rolling through him—only this time it was directed at Trammel. He'd roomed with the asshole for three years; you'd think the bastard would know him by now.

"Relax, Mother—" he snapped. "I'm headed to Kait's."

As he pivoted back to the door and yanked it open, he heard Trammel's relieved grunt sound behind him.

Each step toward his car introduced a new set of aches. By the time he'd unlocked his Mustang and gingerly eased his protesting body inside, he was more interested in a nice, long soak in Kait's shower than hashing things out with Demi.

Tag claimed that nothing had happened between him and Demi the night before. That he'd picked her up, they'd shared a kiss and he'd dropped her off. Now that some of that red-hot mist had faded from Aiden's brain, he believed the bastard too.

Tag might be a poacher, but he wasn't a liar.

Besides, if something had happened between his roommate and Demi the night before Tag would have thrown it at him in the heat of the battle like any good warrior.

Nothing would have hurt like knowing Demi had taken another man into her bed.

Which was the root of the rage he'd directed at Tag. Maybe she hadn't slept with Tag. But that didn't mean she hadn't welcomed some other guy into her bed, or crawled into his. That didn't mean she hadn't trolled the bars before, and picked someone else up. That didn't mean she'd been living like a nun during his last twenty months of deployment.

He swore softly, his fingers rigid around the steering wheel. He'd convinced himself she wasn't ready for a physical relationship, and that he'd be safe leaving her behind—that she'd be there waiting for him when he returned—like Snow White waiting for her regenerating kiss.

It hadn't occurred to him that she might go looking for that kiss on her own.

Nor had he thought to question how he'd get past it if she had.

CHAPTER THREE

Yawning, Demi stepped inside the elevator and leaned over to punch the lobby button. With aggravating slowness the doors closed, and after a subtle lurch, the machine began its slow descent.

Seven thirty in the morning was an ungodly hour to be up and about—or at least it was today, after a restless night spent tossing and turning. What she really needed was a gallon of coffee, or an eight hour nap. Or both. Yawning again, she glanced at her wrist watch. The taxi should be waiting below by now. After she dropped the spare set of keys off with the building superintendent, she'd ask the driver to stop somewhere so she could grab a cup of coffee. Although...she grimaced. Chances were, anywhere the driver stopped would have subpar coffee. It was one of the hazards of owning a gourmet coffee stand—nothing tasted as good as the fare she made herself.

Leaning back against the elevator wall, she yawned again and gave serious consideration to canceling the cab and heading back to bed. She could collect her Volkswagen tomorrow, after brewing enough coffee to prop her eyes open.

The lack of competition for car services was the only advantage to starting the day this early—scratch that, maybe not the *only* advantage. There was another distinct advantage. The bar her Volkswagen was parked in front of was closed. At least she wouldn't have to run the gauntlet of the Tavern's clientele, or the risk of stumbling into one patron in particular.

Which reminded her of a third advantage: she could collect her car and return home without anyone—read, Kait or Aiden—being the wiser about her incredible bout of foolishness the night before.

What the hell were you thinking, Demi?

But that was the whole problem, wasn't it? She hadn't been thinking. She'd let her hormones grab the reins and charge willy-nilly toward sexual fulfillment. A mistake on her part, at least on her rational, sensible, let's-make-decisions with our brain, part. Letting her libido out of the cave and arming it with red had been a dangerous miscalculation. It had proved her hormone-sopped brain had no concept of self-control or rational thinking.

She'd been remarkably lucky. Things could have gone so much worse.

In fact, the night probably would have turned dicey without Brett Taggart's intervention, which she needed to thank him for when he showed up at her door. He seemed like the kind of guy to return a date's purse, and while their interaction the night before didn't exactly fall into the "date," category, she had left her purse in his truck. At some point he was bound to notice it and use her driver's license information to track her down. If not, she'd have to track him down.

She straightened as the elevator bell dinged and the lobby panel lit up. With painful slowness the doors slid open to reveal a muscled bare chest with a totally ripped pair of six-pack abs. Her body signaled its appreciation of the artwork, by straightening and flushing.

Now why couldn't it have reacted to Brett last night with such enthusiasm? She'd bet he had the same muscled chest and abdomen. Maybe that was the key...getting a good look at his naked torso. How politically incorrect would it be to ask him to take his shirt off when he delivered her purse?

It wasn't often fate provided her with such a perfect example of eye candy, so she took a moment to appreciate the sight. Hell's bells, the man was gorgeous—sexier than any of those bare-chested dudes on the legions of romance novels Kait devoured by the sackful.

Her hormones whined, expressing their interest by bombarding her poor spine and belly with an assortment of tingles and chills. Heaven help her, even her palms were sweating. Her gaze traveled up his sculpted body with increasing appreciation—please let his face be just as spectacular!—until they hit the first dusky imprint of an ugly bruise, followed by the first smear of blood.

Whoa...she backed up a bit, and continued her assessment with caution. More bruises shadowed his upper abdomen and lower chest, but it was the next streak of blood that backed her up and extinguished the tingles and chills.

Apparently her hormones and logical brain shared one common characteristic. They were both squeamish at the sight of blood. She was outta here.

She sidled to the right, intending to slip past him. He shifted along with her, blocking her passage, which sent the hair on the back of her neck bolting straight up. *Settle down, Demi. He's not trying to block you in. It was just a coincidence. He simply moved at the same time you did.*

She tried to coax some breath into her lungs with that line of reassurance. A coincidence, that's all. Just a coincidence. He wouldn't deliberately block her exit from the elevator...would he? Sure, a leashed aura of danger surrounded his ripped physique. But he didn't emit the crazy vibe, and he'd have to be considerably crazy to try anything in plain view of the lobby.

Clearing her throat politely, she stepped to the right. He mirrored her movement again, blocking her exit. The slow, deliberate countermove stiffened her shoulders. Her eyebrows snapped together. Okay, now the asshole was just toying with her. Scowling, her gaze shot to his face, only to stumble when it fell across a blood crusted chin. A split, bloody lip came into view next, along with red-rinsed swelling along his right cheekbone.

She winced. Hell's bells, it looked like someone had mistaken this guy's face for a punching bag. He had to be in too much pain to be planning anything nefarious. The injuries to his face could have affected his vision, too. Maybe he hadn't even realized he'd blocked her exit. Feeling more charitable, she lifted her gaze and found herself ensnared by a pair of familiar black eyes—glittering, dangerous black eyes.

Swallowing hard, she took a careful step back, scanning the increasingly familiar face. "Aiden?"

What in the world had happened to him?

He stalked forward, directly toward her, backing her up even further. Once he was on the other side of the elevator doors he stopped and reached for the control panel, jabbing the button with his index finger.

Demi swallowed again. There had been a world of controlled fury in that motion. She scanned his battered face more intently. The injuries were fresh...like, an hour fresh. Obviously Aiden was having a bad day. A *very* bad day—or more likely a very bad morning. She debated reminding him that Kait—his sister—lived on the sixth floor. Except, considering how often he visited Kait, he knew where she lived. Then again, maybe the blows to his head had addled his brain a bit.

Should I offer to play nursemaid?

The primitive part of her brain concerned with sex and all things that led to sexual arousal jumped up and down with both metaphorical feet and squealed a resounding *YES! YES! PLEASE!* But the cautious hemisphere of her brain studied the leashed frustration and fury on his face and decided to pass him off to Kait. The elevator bell dinged, reminding Demi that she still had a taxi waiting and a car to collect.

"Well, I gotta run. Remember—Kait lives on the sixth floor, not the fifth," she said, stepping to the right. "Number 607," she added, just in case the beating he'd taken had jarred more than the floor number loose.

Instead of correcting the floor choice, he shifted to the right, blocking her exit again.

Frustrated, Demi stopped to glare. "I don't have time to play these games, you asshole. Let me through." The elevator doors started to close, and she glared harder. "I'm serious, Aiden, I'm in a hurry."

"Yeah?" He raised a pitch-black eyebrow and subtly shifted his weight over his feet as though he were prepared to stand there all day. The doors shut. With a jolt, the elevator started to rise. "Where are you headed without your driver's license or car?"

Without...

For the first time, she noticed the t-shirt slung over his shoulder and something black and shiny and leather tucked under his left armpit. Something that looked frighteningly like her missing purse.

She groaned beneath her breath.

"It's the perfect size," he said, pure challenge in his glittering black gaze as he grabbed her purse with his left hand and held it aloft like a football.

Don't ask, Demi. Don't ask. Do you really want to know what he's talking about?

It didn't help that he seemed to vibrate at some low-level frequency—like a force field that was about to explode and shower her with sparks.

"To carry a whole party pack of rubbers," he continued, without her participation. "Something to fit everyone." When she didn't respond, he raised his thick black eyebrows even higher. "Just how many guys were you planning on picking up last night?"

His question dropped into the elevator like a dare. Or maybe a threat.

She could hardly pretend she didn't recognize the purse, or know what he was talking about. Her driver's license was in that purse, and from his fixation on the condoms, there was little doubt that he'd opened the damn thing and recognized who it belonged by her license.

Coughing to clear her throat, she sighed. "You know Brett."

He smiled grimly. "My roommate."

Oh wow...just...wow. Did she know how to pick her partners in crime, or what? She'd suspected they might know each other...but roommates? How humiliatingly unfortunate. She'd never told Brett who she was looking for, but Aiden was an intelligent guy—he'd probably figured it out.

Her cheeks turned into a blast furnace, emitting so much heat she could feel it burning down her neck. "Look, I don't know what Brett told you, but—"

"He took you home." Grimness bonded to accusation, and hardened his voice and face in concert.

She shuffled her feet, grimacing, her face getting hotter and hotter. She could hardly deny the accusation. Her purse had been found in Brett's truck.

"Well, yeah, and I left my purse in his truck, but—"

"You kissed him."

Demi stopped to stare. Was it her imagination, or had his

body actually swelled by a couple of inches at that last comment? She shook her head, brushing the impression aside. Her imagination was certainly working overtime this morning.

"Yeah, well..." She stumbled into silence. This conversation was clearly headed for embarrassing territory. Time to jump ship—or in this case, elevator—and live to be embarrassed another day. She edged around him to the control panel, but the elevator dinged before she even touched it, and began to slow. "Well, thanks for bringing my purse over, but I really have to go. I have a cab waiting to take me to my car."

"Cancel it." His voice was autocratic. "I'll take you over to pick it up."

"No offense, but you aren't taking me anywhere looking like that," she snapped back, making sure her voice was every bit as dictatorial as his had been. "Everyone will assume I've been kidnapped by a serial killer."

He scowled and looked down. "It's not that bad."

Demi rocked back on her heels, rounding her eyes in exaggerated shock. "Have you looked in the mirror recently? I'm surprised you weren't pulled over on your way over here. You look like someone put you through a meat grinder."

Okay, maybe he didn't look *that* bad, but she had no intension of hanging out with him on the half-hour trip over to pick up her car. For some reason her meeting with Brett and her purse full of condoms had chapped his ass big time. She could just feel a lecture coming on. A big brother kind of lecture. The kind she'd heard him give Kait on numerous occasions. And it would be beyond humiliating to endure a lecture on sexual safety from the very guy she'd intended to track down and tempt into sexual shenanigans.

The elevator doors slowly rolled open.

"After I've cleaned up, and we've had a conversation," he

clarified, irritation still crackling in his eyes. "I'll run you out to pick up your car."

"Thanks for the offer, but I have other plans, and we don't have anything to talk about." She tried to walk around him, but he blocked her again.

"Hey, what do you think you're doing?" This time the protest didn't come from her. It came from Chester, who was standing on the other side of the open elevator door. Chester was her best coffee customer—a tall, stork-like man who lived on the third floor and hit on her daily with all the awkward intensity of an agoraphobic introvert. He blinked at them, rocking nervously back and forth, as though he couldn't decide whether to charge forward or back up. "Are you okay, Demi?"

Before she had a chance to respond, Aiden hit the close door button. "She's fine, and this elevator's full."

"Now wait a minute," Chester said, bobbing his head and blinking his eyes in unison, a nervous tick of his that had the unfortunate effect of making him look more stork-like than ever. An impression further enhanced by his long, thin honker of a nose.

She could see the sheen of anxiety in his olive-colored eyes and instinctively sought to reassure him. "I'm fine, Chester," she said as the doors started to close. "This is Aiden, Kait's brother."

"Well, that's all well and good, but—"

The door shut and started to rise. But before it reached the next floor, Aiden punched the emergency stop button.

"What are you doing?" Demi's voice rose as sheer frustration flooded her. He'd effectively caged her. Now she'd have to listen to his brewing lecture. *Damn it.*

"You don't want to talk," he reminded her, something dark and dangerous and...sexy in his voice. "So we'll just have to find another way to communicate."

She took a cautious step back, eyeing him warily. "Look, it's none of your business what I do, where I go, or what I have in my purse."

"I'm making it my business," he said, stalking toward her with determined steps.

In no time she found her back flush against the wall of the elevator while chills raged up and down her spine and butter-flies exploded in her belly. Her eyes widened as he leaned over her, bracing his left palm against the wall next to her shoulder.

"Look," she sputtered, bracing her palm against his chest as his right hand rose to cup her chin. "There's obviously been some kind of a misunderstanding here."

"No misunderstanding," he murmured, his lips hovering a hair's breadth from her mouth. "You have a purse full of condoms and no one to use them on. I'm offering my services."

Wha...wha...what?

Had he just said what she thought he'd said? Or were her ears playing tricks on her?

Her head swam as his scent—a hot earthy musk with the slightest metallic undercurrent—flooded her lungs and fogged her brain. Hell's bells, he smelled so good...like hot, vital male. But he felt even better, his chest hard and hot against her hand. The steady thump of his heart against her palm acted like a shot of pure adrenaline, spiking her own heartbeat and breathing.

He brushed his lips over hers once, as though he was conducting some kind of test—which she must have passed, because he settled his mouth over hers.

Hell's b—he was kissing her!

She wouldn't have believed it, except his tongue had snuck inside her mouth and was doing all sorts of wicked things inside there...wicked, delicious things—like stroking her tongue and the inside of her cheeks and sucking every bit of oxygen from her brain.

Her mind went woozy, and her muscles limp. She leaned

forward, pressing her body full length against his. He dropped the arm he'd braced against the wall, and wrapping it around her waist, dragged her even closer, until they were pressed shoulder to shoulder and thigh to thigh.

It quickly became evident that he hadn't been joking about making use of those condoms. In fact, from the feel of his mouth on hers, and his penis pressing against her belly, he was quite enthusiastic about the offer.

She'd spent months dreaming about him, but the reality burned every one of those erotic dreams from her mind. His body was hot and hard against her, rigid muscles sheathed in fire...fire that burned through her skin and sparked an answering flame within her. Her arms lifted, circling his thick neck. She pressed in closer and closer, her mouth moving urgently beneath his. And then, suddenly, he hissed and jerked back.

Off balance, her muscles weak and shaking, she almost dropped to her knees. Would have, if not for the arm he still had wrapped around her waist. He waited until her legs started working again before dropping his arm and stepping back. A broad hand rose to his mouth. Her lethargic gaze followed it.

Her foggy brain clicked into focus after discovering his lip was more swollen than ever and a fresh trickle of blood dribbled down the corner of his mouth. She winced, watching him swipe a hand over the oozing trickle. She'd completely forgotten about his injuries, hadn't even felt the swelling against her mouth. Lord, as painful as that split lip looked, it was amazing he'd kissed her at all.

Slowly her gaze drifted up to his eyes. They weren't glittering anymore. Rather they were hard with an angry disgusted sheen. Luckily, none of this new, negative energy seemed to be directed at her.

"I need to clean up," he said, his grim gaze flickering between her lips and eyes.

"Okay. "She licked her bottom lip nervously beneath his frowning gaze and a sweet, slightly metallic taste spread through her mouth. "What's wrong?"

"I'm bleeding all over you." A frown settled over his face.

Bleeding all over...

She licked her lips again, and then his answer registered. She froze. Good God —that's what that sweet, metallic taste was. His blood.

Ewwwwww.

She made a face and hastily scrubbed at her mouth.

"I hope you don't have AIDS or something," she said, more to be a smartass than because she was actually concerned about the possibility.

Kait had said that the SEAL program required constant medical and physical exams of their warriors. And Aiden seemed like a pretty careful guy, the kind of guy who'd make sure to protect himself. Besides, she couldn't lay all the blame on him. She'd seen his split, bleeding lip. Common sense dictated that his blood would transfer to her during a kiss—information, evidently, her hormone-saturated brain had sought to suppress.

Clearly, her libido hadn't placed much importance on being infected by tainted blood. Equally clear, her libido needed to be taken out and shot. She'd packed the condoms for a reason; she'd been determined to protect herself, and not just from an unplanned pregnancy.

"I'm clean." He bent to snatch up the t-shirt and purse, which had fallen to the elevator floor at some point during their heated kiss and stepped back, turning to the control panel. He punched the run button this time and the elevator lurched back to life. After hitting the button for the fifth floor, he turned back to her. "What about you?"

"Me?" Taken aback, she simply stared at him. He couldn't

be serious. She'd been married right out of high school, and faithful to her husband both before and after his death.

"You have a purse full of condoms, and from the number of texts hitting my phone this morning, there was a bar full of men last night volunteering to model those condoms for you." There was a grim, tense note in his voice. Ignoring the elevator's chime, he tilted his head and studied her face intently. "How often do you troll bars like that?"

Trolling...number of texts?

"Texts?" she repeated faintly. "Your buddies were texting you about *me*?"

He shrugged. "More about Tag. It's been a while since he's seen any action." His voice tightened. "How often are you hitting the bars, Demi?

She swallowed. What the hell? If anything did happen between them, he'd find out how inexperienced she was. While she and Donnie had shared an active love life, by no stretch of the imagination had it been an adventurous one.

"Last night was the first," she admitted.

His seemed to relax at that, but it was so infinitesimal she wasn't sure whether she'd actually seen it, or whether it had been her imagination. The door slid open, and he stepped out, holding it open for her to follow.

"Do your buddies know who I am?" she asked, squirming at the thought of all his friends knowing her name. Although why it should matter was beyond her. It wasn't like she was going to run into any of them again anytime soon.

"No." He shot her the strangest look. "What's with this red outfit you wore last night?"

She stopped in her tracks, which just happened to be in front of her condo door.

"You heard about that?" she asked, absently pulling her spare set of keys from her pocket.

"That outfit was the topic of most of the texts," he said absently. Apparently she was taking too long to open the door, because he passed the purse to her and took the keys from her hand, cast one quick look over them and inserted the correct one in the lock. "You're gonna have to wear it for me sometime." He shot her another of those glittering, hungry looks. "Sometime soon."

Well, how about that? Her brain science experiment on male arousal had proved remarkably effective. He hadn't even seen the slutty red outfit; apparently just hearing about it had been enough to lower his inhibitions and propel him to seek her out.

As he ushered her through her condo door and closed it behind them, it suddenly occurred to her that she was all alone in her condo with an almost naked Aiden, and that he clearly expected things to get very physical between them very fast.

Those damn butterflies took flight in her belly again. Her scalp started to tingle and her palms sweat—only none of these symptoms carried the earlier heat of arousal. They carried the tension of nerves instead.

How ridiculous was that? She'd gone out of her way to attract his attention last night, only to return home depressed and disappointed that nothing had come from her efforts. And now that he was actually here, in her condo, and perfectly willing to engage in the kind of sexual shenanigans she'd been craving for the past year, she was getting cold feet?

Where the hell was her libido when she needed it?

CHAPTER FOUR

She smelled like roses.

Aiden filled his lungs with her scent as he followed her through the condo's front door. He'd noticed the distinct floral aroma in the elevator, but hadn't realized that the scent was coming from her, at least not until he'd moved in for the kiss. Not that his dick had cared where the floral smell was coming from. The moment he stepped into the elevator and got that first whiff of roses, his cock had sat up and whined—as usual. To his confusion, a couple years back the damn thing had latched onto that particular scent like Pavlov's dog had latched onto the bell. He sure as hell hadn't understood or appreciated the peculiar reaction at the time.

A grin tugged at the corners of his mouth, but the pull against his split lip hurt too much to maintain the expression for long. At least he finally had an explanation for this ramped up reaction to roses. At some point in the past his subconscious must have linked his attraction to Demi to that particular scent, and boom—the smell of roses equaled an instant erection.

"Let's get some ice on that lip," Demi said, her voice all business. She sped up, pulling away from the hand he'd rested against the small of her back. Aiden increased his pace to keep up, but slowed again when the extension in his stride pulled at his abdomen and chest until the bruised flesh burned.

"A frozen veggie package will work," Aiden called after her, studying her stiff back thoughtfully.

Her muscles, which had been pliant and soft against his chest in the elevator, had tensed with each step toward her condo. By the time he'd opened her door, she'd been as rigid as steel against his hand. Now she was racing down the hall like a dozen tangos with flash grenades were locked on her tail.

Sure looked like his Demi was having a serious attack of cold feet.

Oddly enough, her sudden reservations were soothing rather than frustrating, and some of the tension inside him eased. While she'd claimed the night before had been her first foray into the bar scene, he hadn't been sure he could trust that declaration. Would she admit it if she'd been making the rounds on a regular basis? She must have sensed his rage at the thought of her picking up another man. What if she'd simply given him the answer he'd clearly wanted to hear?

Except she wasn't acting like a woman who'd plowed her way through the barracks. Once she'd roused from that kiss, she'd launched into pure skittishness, which pointed to a certain lack of experience. Now that he had her where he needed her—alone, and inside her condo—he could afford to back off. Let her settle down. Let her get used to him being underfoot, and then seduce her into taking that first step toward him of her own volition.

No sense in pressing her and scaring her off.

So he lingered on his way down the hall to study the stark black and white photos lining the calming mint-colored walls. The pictures alternated between photos of old, dilapidated barns and the facial portraits of people in the twilight of their lives—faces that wore their years in the creases and folds etched upon their flesh. Absently working the stiff, throbbing fingers of his right hand, he wandered from photograph to photograph, admiring the artistic use of light and shadow, before stepping into the living room and stopping to stare.

The woman liked color, that was for sure. The minty green of the hallway gave way to peach in the living room, although the carpet remained a rich deep green. The color scheme was both chaotic and striking, rather like its mistress's pink hair. The walls looked freshly painted and the carpet brand new. Both were a startling departure from the last time he'd been in here.

Which had been what? Three years ago? He'd only been in the condo once before, back when he'd toured it prior to purchasing it for her. Donnie had barely been gone a week, and he'd been desperate to make sure she was safe before he shipped out for his imminent deployment. A condo one flight down from his supportive, but bossy sister had been just the ticket.

The *gift*—as Kait called the...talent...he'd inherited from his Arapaho ancestors—showered him with more money than he'd be able to spend in his lifetime. So the money he'd shelled out for this place had been recouped within a couple of months.

Hell, it had cost almost as much in bribes to funnel the condo and bogus inheritance Demi's way without her getting suspicious of where the sudden windfall had come from. But as far as he could tell, she'd never questioned the foundation of her inheritance, or whether Donnie had really kept their sudden good fortune quiet in order to surprise her with it on their seventh anniversary, had he lived to celebrate it with her.

Knowing that Demi was living in such close proximity to his sister and that Kait had stepped up to help her through her grief had made that first fourteen month rotation bearable. Nothing had made the next twenty months bearable. Toward the end, all he could think about was how Donnie had been gone almost three years, and at some point she was bound to wake up and realize she was still a vibrant, sexual woman capable of opening her heart to another man. He'd been determined to be that man, which was impossible when he was half way around the world.

Thank Christ he was home now, ready to stake his claim, and from the look of things, right in the nick of time, too. Now he just needed to ease into her life as quickly as possible, then into her bed, and finally into her heart.

He glanced toward the kitchen, where Demi had disappeared. The condo was one of those open concept plans where the kitchen was open to the living room. In this case, a waist-high counter which also served as a breakfast bar separated the two. He couldn't see her from his vantage point, but the silence that had fallen between them was so thick it was almost palpable. Frowning, he followed her into the kitchen. He didn't want to crowd her, but giving her too much space could cause problems, too—entrench her in this sudden bout of nerves.

"Demi?" he asked quietly, on catching sight of her.

She'd opened the freezer door and was just standing there, staring inside the compartment. Her shoulders stiffened at the sound of his voice, and she took a deep breath and exhaled slowly. Reaching inside the freezer, she grabbed a white plastic bag and dragged it out.

"Take a seat and I'll clean that lip." Her voice was brisk as she stepped back from the fridge and closed the freezer door with calm deliberation.

Given a mirror and a sink, he could take care of the cleanup himself. But her offer carried more than simple nursing. It offered proximity. To make good on her promise, she'd have to sit close enough to touch him. And skin on skin contact was the fastest way to build intimacy. He headed for the round table tucked into the octagonal alcove next to the kitchen and pulled out a chair. Turning it until it faced left, he sat down.

She bustled to the sink with her make-shift icepack and turned on the tap. After grabbing a couple of kitchen towels from one drawer, and a square white tin with the red symbol of a first aid kit from another, she turned back to the faucet and stuck a towel under the flow of water. Turning the tap off, she wrung the towel out and collected her supplies.

"All I have is Brussels sprouts," she said dropping the white plastic bag onto the glass table. The metal first aid tin she set down with more care.

"That'll do." Aiden took a deep breath, wanting to bask in the sweet scent of roses enveloping him, but the burning pain that rode his torso as his chest expanded distracted him. His cock, on the other hand, launched into a full-fledged salute once it got a whiff of that floral smell. Apparently nothing could distract it.

When she finally took her seat they were pressed knee to knee. He waited a few seconds for her to move forward. When she didn't, he scooted his chair to the right—grimacing as the pain quadrupled in his abdomen—until his legs could slip between hers.

Her face went rosy, but she didn't push herself back. Instead, she leaned forward and began dabbing at his chin. She started low, well below his split lip or the knot on his cheek, so the pain was minimal. He relaxed beneath the gentle brush of the warm wet cloth.

"You never told me how this happened," she murmured, as she stroked the cloth across his chin and down his neck.

He grunted in response and tilted his head back to give her more access. But even that slight stretch pinched at his swollen, painful mouth. He swore beneath his breath. With luck, the warm, damp cloth would loosen the tight flesh, because he had plans for his mouth—and they didn't include talking.

"So?" she prompted, scooting closer until she was perched

on the edge of her chair. She braced a palm against the top of his thigh and leaned in even closer.

His head dropped, and he studied her face. Her cheeks were even rosier and she was avoiding his gaze. She knew exactly where she'd put her hand, as well as the implied intimacy of the touch.

Thank Christ. She was getting her nerves back.

Her face was still flushed as she leaned in and gently pressed the wet, warm cloth against the corner of his mouth. He trapped a hiss behind his locked jaw as a thousand wasps attacked his lip in unison. Son of a bitch that hurt—which didn't bode well for his plans.

"I take it you're not going to tell me?" she asked.

What the hell was she talking about? He cast his mind back over the admittedly one-sided conversation. Oh, yeah, she'd asked about his injuries. He frowned, and then shrugged. What the hell, she'd asked.

"Tag and I had a disagreement over the events of last night," he told her in a dry voice.

The pressure against his lip eased slightly as she drew back. "Tag?"

"Brett Taggart? My roommate? The guy you let take you home last night?" There was more sharpness in the response than he'd intended.

She picked up on the tone immediately, and her eyebrows snapped together. She pressed the cloth back against his mouth with decidedly more pressure than before, but eased it back the instant he grunted and pulled away.

"I already told you, nothing happened," she snapped, and the red flagging her cheeks this time had more to do with irritation than nerves. "And, may I remind you, it's none of your damn business who I let take me home," she added, pure annoyance crackling through the declaration.

He wanted to argue about that, but she was right. He had no claim to her. At least at the moment. Soon, though. Very soon. He backed off with a grunt of acknowledgement.

Slight as it was, that acknowledgement was enough to appease her. She leaned in again, but this time, instead of pressing the wet cloth to his mouth, she began dabbing at it.

Jesus Christ!

He jerked back. What the fuck? Had she swapped out the dishrag for a handful of stinging nettles? When she leaned in to press the washcloth to his lip again, he caught her hand and tried to take it away, but the swollen, stiff fingers of his right hand refused to bend, or grasp.

She got the message, though, and lowered the wash cloth to the table. Aiden twisted to grab the Brussels sprouts with his left hand, and caught his breath as pain lanced through his abdomen. Ah, damn—he regulated his breathing until the ache eased.

"Ice will help the most," he said after a minute, not wanting her to think he didn't appreciate her ministrations.

Carefully shifting back to face her, he eased the make-shift ice pack over his mouth. The cold went to work immediately, and the stinging vanished as numbness crept across his mouth.

"I hear kissing works too," she announced, out of the blue. "Rumor has it that kissing makes *everything* better."

His gaze shot to her face. That rosy flush of uncertainty had invaded her cheeks again, but her brown eyes were steady as they held his—inviting.

He wasn't an idiot. No way in hell was he turning that offer down.

"I've heard the same." He dropped the ice pack onto the table.

She tried for a sophisticated smile, but he could see the nerves returning to her eyes. Without giving her time for second thoughts, he leaned forward, only to catch his breath as pain crimped his chest and upper abdomen. Freezing, he slipped his left hand around the nape of her neck, and drew her toward him instead. She came easily, settling her lips against his.

The kiss was gentle—too damn gentle; practically non-existent. The lightest brush of lips against lips. Maybe. All he could feel was a light tingling pressure against his numb mouth. His swollen, stiff fingers slid up, tangling in her spiky hair, which was surprising soft against his palm. He pulled her closer, desperate for a taste of her.

"Aow." She jerked back, pulling her head away from his frozen claw.

"Sorry," he muttered, lowering his arm. He needed to get some ice on his hand, too. It was pretty much useless in its current condition.

She leaned in again, without his urging this time, and for a split second, he felt something—the softest, sweetest brush of satin against his swollen mouth. And then the hornets of the damned attached themselves to his lip and stung the hell out of him.

"Son of a bitch!" He jerked back so hard he almost toppled his chair, and then seized up for a good ten seconds while his chest and stomach screamed in pain.

Jesus Christ!

When he could move again, he picked the ice pack up and eased it back over his lip.

"Well," she said, leaning back in her chair. "I'll try not to take that personally." The wry tone in her voice told him she wasn't particularly upset.

She turned her attention to his cheek, but the moment the warm, wet cloth settled over the knot on his cheekbone, his whole skull throbbed. Grunting, he jerked his head back and grabbed for the cloth, only to knock it from her hand.

It landed with a wet plop in between their spread knees. Scooting her chair back she bent forward to pick it back up.

His cock twitched, signaling its enthusiasm with a hard, urgent surge of blood as her mouth descended toward his lap. Totally oblivious to the throbbing part of his anatomy that was begging for her attention, she straightened, washcloth in hand, and eyed his chest.

"Well, I can at least wash the blood off your chest. That shouldn't hurt too much."

Famous last words, as it turned out, since even the lightest caress of the wet cloth against the skin of his abdomen and chest burned. He kept his mouth shut, but flinched with each brush of the cloth.

With a huff of frustration she sat back. "Is there any place you don't hurt?"

"Yeah, below my belt." The words escaped without any input from his brain and just hung there.

Her face went brick red, but by God she held her ground. "You're in no condition for below the belt games."

Hell, she might be right about that, regardless of what that little bastard dancing around in his pants wanted him to believe.

"Give me an hour and I'll be *up* for any game you choose," he countered. A half-hour with the ice pack and a half hour in her shower should set him up just fine. Hell, his cock was already up for some action; too bad the rest of his body didn't have the follow through.

She sat back in her chair, a flirty little grin playing around her lips. "I thought SEALs were indestructible. That a gunshot wound wouldn't even slow you down. That you could get beat to hell during the day and pass out multiple orgasms to your womenfolk at night."

He choked at that piece of nonsense. God help him, had she

been reading his sister's romance novels? Talk about an unrealistic view of his profession.

"You've been watching too many Die Hard movies."

"I bet Bruce Willis could kiss me properly with or without a busted lip," she said, her eyes sparkling.

"There's a big difference between Bruce Willis and me," he told her, raising an eyebrow in challenge.

"He makes like a million times more money than you?"

Aiden swallowed a smirk. For accuracy's sake, that statement should have been reversed. But that wasn't what he'd been getting at. "He's not the one about to give you multiple orgasms."

She choked, and then slowly turned in her chair to survey the kitchen, as though she were looking for someone. "He isn't? Then who is? Because judging by the way you flinch every time I touch you, and jerk back every time you try to kiss me—that sure ain't going to be you."

Touché.

He settled back in his chair striving for a smug expression, which was difficult to pull off when half his face was covered by an icepack. "A handful of aspirin and I'm good as new."

Her snort clearly expressed her opinion of *that* piece of fiction. But then a thoughtful look crossed her face. "I should call Kait."

He wanted to believe she was still joking around, but her face looked far too serious for comfort. "Why the hell would you want to do that?" Having Kait underfoot would derail all his plans.

"Because she'd help you a lot more than those icepacks."

Freezing, he eyed her closely. That sounded like she knew about the gift his sister had inherited from her half of their Arapaho genes. Which was new—she hadn't been aware of Kait's talent prior to this last rotation.

Knowing Kait, and her penchant for privacy, she wouldn't have spilled the beans about her ability to heal by touch unless it had been absolutely necessary. Which meant Demi must have been hurt at some point during the past twenty months. And hurt badly enough for Kait to step in and offer to help—or at least try to help.

Absolutely still, his body suddenly cold, he scanned her. No scars, at least none that he could see. And she seemed to move fine...his gaze settled on her head. She'd sheared her head in the last twenty months—and dyed her hair that striking pink. Had there been a reason behind the drastic new hair style?

"You know about Kait's...gift?" he asked slowly.

"Yeah." Her hand absently rose to the nape of her neck and her fingers dug in for a quick massage. "I was in a car accident a year or so ago. Whiplash. It really did a number on me. Kait was a miracle worker."

He didn't realize he was grinding his teeth until pain shot through his jaw. She'd been hurt and he hadn't known it. In pain and he hadn't been around to take care of her. Why in the hell hadn't Kait let him know Demi had been hurt? He could have taken an emergency leave. He would have been in-house to help her. Why hadn't Kait called?

But after a second he shook his head with a scowl. He'd been careful to make sure nobody picked up on his feelings for Demi. Kait wouldn't have known he'd cared one way or the other.

"When you were in the hospital for all those weeks with that injury to your spine, Kait fixed you, right?" Demi raised her eyebrows. "Which means you're in the thirty percent she can heal. Why not let her take the swelling and bruising away?" She sent him an intent, meaningful look. "The sooner you can touch me without flinching, the faster you can back up those wild claims you made."

She meant the multiple orgasms he'd promised her. He wanted to grin, but even the slightest stretch of his lips eighty-sixed that impulse.

"Kait's healing doesn't happen overnight," he reminded her.

If Demi had been on the receiving end of his sister's gift, she knew it took numerous massages for Kait's talent to prove effective. It had taken weeks before Kait's healing ability had put him back on his feet after that disaster in Baghdad.

"The ice and aspirin will work just as fast." He paused to frown, before adding. "Those healings take a lot out of her. She's exhausted, often for hours afterwards. There's no sense in putting her through that when scrapes and bruises will heal on their own in a day or so."

All of which was true, but not the main reason he wanted to avoid Kait's interference. If his sister arrived, he could kiss goodbye any chance of getting Demi to himself for an extended length of time. It was damn near impossible to forge a sense of intimacy with a third wheel underfoot. For the moment, at least, Demi had shed her inhibitions and seemed willing to take the sizzle between them to its natural conclusion. But with Kait interrupting them, Demi's previous bout of cold feet could easily come back into play. For this slow seduction of his to work, he needed Demi to himself, with no outside distractions shoving a wedge between them.

CHAPTER FIVE

Scowling, Demi dug her shoulders into the back rest of her arm chair and glared at the long, broad, frustratingly masculine frame sprawled across her sofa. She'd lost track of how many nights she'd been plagued with steamy, erotic dreams featuring the man sound asleep on her couch. In none of those dreams had Aiden downed a handful of aspirin, slapped icepacks over his face and passed out after a kiss.

If you could even call that a kiss.

Sure, lips had touched...for all of a second or two, before he'd flinched and jerked away. But there hadn't been much plea-sure attached to that fleeting caress—on either of their sides. She sighed morosely, her gaze lingering on his face, or at least what she could see of it. Had the swelling gone down? It was hard to tell with the frozen Brussels sprout bags covering his face. It was even harder to fall into passion when your partner flinched, hissed, or bolted away every time you touched him.

She stared at her hard bound, signed copy of **The King** sitting on the coffee table beside the couch and considered picking it up and giving him a swift smack with it.

There were some men who knew how to treat their ladies right—with multiple orgasms all night, every night. They didn't come home from a hard night on the streets to moan and flinch every time their lovers touched them. Her lips twitched wryly. Of course, they weren't exactly men, and according to lore, vampires healed extraordinarily fast. Plus—well, they didn't actually exist, now did they? Except, possibly, in countless fertile imaginations.

Her frown returned as she stared at the book. The warriors of the Black Dagger Brotherhood were extremely possessive of their women. Admittedly, there was something erotically thrilling about that—in fiction.

In real life, though...

Thoughtful, she turned her attention back to the man sprawled out, dead to the world, in front of her. According to him, the split lip and bruised cheek, not to mention all those bruises along his chest and abdomen, had been delivered during a fight.

A fight over her.

Some women might get a kick out of two good-looking, lethal men fighting over them. She wasn't one of those women. What was titillating in fiction held much less excitement in real life. In fact, the brawl he'd gotten into was disturbing on multiple levels.

For one thing, he'd actually been injured. Granted, the wounds were minor—hardly life threatening—but right now, at this moment, he was in pain...because of her. That didn't sit well at all. She didn't want to be the cause of anyone's pain.

But there was something else that was even more worrisome, something that left a nagging sense of unease.

Why, exactly, had he gotten into that fight? What had propelled him?

Fighting over someone indicated an emotional attachment to the subject of the brawl. After all, nobody would fight over someone they didn't care about.

Her brow furrowed as she rolled that around in her mind.

Sure, there were certain situations where a man, particularly a man with a protective streak, might get into a fight over a woman without actually having any strong feelings for her—like if he was protecting her from a bully or threat.

But that hadn't been the reason behind this fight. In fact, by Aiden's own account, they'd fought specifically because Brett had taken her home. Obviously, Aiden had been under the mistaken impression that his roommate had done a lot more than simply drop her off at her front door. And therein lay the crux of her problem.

Didn't his reaction over that mistaken assumption, a reaction that had led to a fist fight, indicate some depth of feeling? Why would he get so angry, unless he cared that his roommate had taken her home and spent the night doing a lot more than sleeping with her? Maybe Brett had made some comment about her that Aiden had taken exception to—but even that explanation indicated some level of emotional attachment. Words carried no power, unless feelings were involved.

Besides, she couldn't imagine Brett saying anything Aiden would find offensive. Granted, their interaction had been fleeting, but he'd come across as far too much of a gentleman to kiss and tell.

And then there was Aiden's demeanor in the elevator. Certainly anger had been spilling off of him, but there had been something else there, too, something like possessiveness. Which also implied he'd formed an emotional attachment to her. When he'd formed this attachment was another big question. The man hadn't seemed to notice she'd existed prior to today.

Granted, most of that impression was based on her interaction with him while she'd been married. While she'd been attracted to him, albeit with no intention of acting on that attraction, he hadn't appeared to be equally attracted to her. Nor had he treated her differently after Donnie's death, although they hadn't spent much time together after she'd been widowed. He'd spent most of those three years out on deployment.

She frowned, thinking back. During that black haze of grief and disbelief following the freak accident that had killed her husband, she vaguely remembered Aiden being constantly underfoot. He'd been the one to untangle the insurance policies, and help her through the unbelievable amount of paperwork and decisions following Donnie's death.

If it hadn't been for Aiden and Kait's support, she would have crumbled. She didn't remember much of those early weeks. Nothing had seemed real. She'd drifted through the days and nights in denial, trapped in a hazy nightmare.

Maybe she wouldn't have had such a hard time accepting that Donnie was gone, if his death had happened differently—like in a car accident, or a heart attack, or the slow destruction of cancer. Those were possibilities you heard about every day. But to lose someone you loved to a foul ball, at a company-sponsored baseball game? How often did that happen?

One moment Donnie had been sitting there beside her on the steel bleachers, teasing her about the latest vampire romance novel she'd been reading, and the next he was gone. It just hadn't seemed real, hadn't seemed possible.

She sighed, glancing around the condo. If only he'd told her right away about the inheritance he'd gotten from his uncle Benito, instead of waiting until he'd bought the condo so he could surprise her with it on their anniversary. If he'd told her immediately, they could have moved into the condo together and she'd have memories of him in here. Memories of him beside her in bed, cooking in the kitchen, or cuddling her on the couch while they watched one of those detective shows he'd enjoyed so much.

But it had been just like Donnie to wait to surprise her. He'd loved doing such unexpected things, and he'd known how much she loved Kait's condo. So he'd given up his dream of a house so he could buy her the luxury condominium he knew she'd coveted. And he'd done it in such a way she couldn't protest—couldn't insist that they buy a house instead, as was his dream.

That was her Donnie, generous to a fault.

Of course, the fact he'd never shared the condo with her did make it easier in some respects. Since there were no memories of him here, it didn't feel like a betrayal to invite another man into her home, and quite possibly her bed.

If memories of Donnie had clung to this place, it might not be as enticing watching the long, broad masculine body sprawled across the suede cushions of her couch. He'd been sleeping for—she glanced at the decorative oval clock tucked in the corner of the bookcase—thirty minutes.

How much longer was he going to sleep? While the taxi she'd summoned earlier was probably long gone, she could call for another one and run over to San Diego to pick her car up. He might not even awaken before she returned. There was no sense in just sitting here and staring at him while he slept.

Decision made, she pushed herself to her feet.

"Where you headed?" Aiden mumbled, before she'd even taken that first step away from the chair.

He hadn't bothered to lift the makeshift icepack from his mouth, but the question was clearly audible anyway.

"I thought I'd take care of some chores while you slept."

"I'm not asleep," he said, reaching up to rescue the icepack that was slipping off his mouth.

She shrugged. "Then while you rest."

He opened the eye that wasn't covered by the vegetable pack he'd slapped across his cheek and pinned her with an intense black gaze. "I told you I'd take you to pick up your car."

"Yes, you did." Demi cocked her head and stared at him with determination. "However, you obviously need the rest and more time with the ice."

He plucked the white plastic bags off his face, and gingerly sat up before swinging his legs over the side of the couch. "These need to go back in the freezer anyway. The vegetables are melting." He grunted softly as he stood up. "Look, just point me to the shower, give me ten minutes to soak, and I'll run you over to get your car."

She frowned as she studied him. His face actually looked worse after the icing. The cold had turned patches of his skin an angry red, but beneath the crimson she could see the mottled shadow of early bruising. And from the care with which he'd sat and then stood, his torso was also feeling the effect of being mistaken for a punching bag.

"Shouldn't you ice the bruising on your torso and abdomen rather than soaking in hot water? Won't the heat make the bruises worse?" She stepped closer, and inched aside the ripped shirt to get a look at his chest and abdomen.

The bruises there were much more pronounced than the ones on his face. Maybe the icing had helped after all...or maybe there was more going on with his torso than simple bruising. "Are you sure you didn't crack a rib or something? Maybe you should see a doctor?"

"This is nothing compared to a cracked rib." His dark eyes softened as they stared steadily back at her. "Trust me; I've survived much worse."

Demi swallowed hard. She didn't doubt that for a moment. He was in a pretty high-risk profession. Not just high-risk for injuries, but high-risk for death. That risk was one of the reasons she needed to keep her libido separate from her emotions when it came to him.

A no strings, no emotions, lots-of-sex relationship...that's what she was looking for.

She flashed back to his earlier hint of possessiveness in the elevator. And the anger he'd displayed at the thought of Brett taking her home. They needed to have a discussion about where things were headed before they let this progress any further.

"You could join me in the shower," he said, a wicked gleam sliding through his eyes. "I'll even let you wash my..." He lifted and waggled his eyebrows at her. "...back. I promise to return the favor."

Except his gaze dropped to her chest, a silent admission of where he was imagining washing.

With a roll of her eyes, Demi stepped away. Somehow, showering with a man always ended with squeaky clean boobs.

"And here I thought you'd be more imaginative," she said dryly. "I can wash my breasts myself, thank you very much."

"I didn't say I was going to stop there." Aiden's voice was equally dry as he slowly slid his gaze down her body, the glitter in his eyes growing more pronounced by the second. He stopped when he reached her hips and a hungry expression touched his face.

To Demi's surprise, a tingle swept her spine and damp warmth pooled between her thighs. She snorted in disbelief. Her libido was beyond desperate, if that slow perusal had turned it on.

"I'm betting you're no more up for shower games than below the belt games," Demi retorted, but she couldn't stop the smile from escaping. The man was certainly determined, she'd give him that.

"Trust me," he said with a slow, suggestive grin. "I'm completely *up* for either."

Well, you certainly walked into that one.

She swallowed a smirk. Of course he'd made it impossible not to check out his self-proclaimed state of *"upness"*. She didn't even bother fighting the impulse to drop her gaze. Instead, she narrowed her eyes, tilted her head, and pasted an assessing expression on her face as she zeroed in on his crotch.

Oh my...

She barely caught herself from fanning her face with her fingers. "That's some pretty aggressive swelling you got going on..." She raised her head, keeping her face as deadpan as possible. "Perhaps some ice might be helpful down there?"

His laugh caught on a wince and he touched a finger to his bottom lip.

"I doubt ice will do a damn thing. The little bastard has no common sense." With an exaggerated sigh, he dropped his arm. "Fine, if you won't *help* me in the shower, could you at least help me get undressed?" He held up his right hand, with its swollen, scrapped knuckles. "I can barely bend my fingers."

*Impressive...*Demi bit back a laugh. He'd actually managed to make himself look pathetic and helpless—or at least as helpless as a six-foot-plus combat warrior in prime physical condition could look.

"You have *two* hands," she reminded him, chewing on the inside of her lip to stop the giggle from escaping.

She'd forgotten how much fun it was to engage in sexual repartee. Donnie, bless him, used to get so flustered and red-faced, she'd given up on such banter. It had felt cruel to toss sexual innuendoes at him when they made him so uncomfortable.

"But I'm right handed," he told her with a totally straight face.

She knew for a fact the man was ambidextrous. Kait had told her he'd trained as stringently with his left hand as his right, and could wield a knife or a gun with equal accuracy no matter which hand he used. He was perfectly capable of undressing right or left handed. Not that she was going to let on that she knew his little secret...

"Oh...well...in that case." She deliberately licked her lips and sidled toward him, her hand rising toward his pelvis.

She trailed her fingers lightly up the bulge in his crotch—which was increasing by the second—on her way to his belt.

It had been a long time since she'd flirted so aggressively with a man. But the circumstances were perfect for it. Regardless of how sexually suggestive the teasing got, he wasn't in any condition to actually act on it. And even if he could perform as promised, he wouldn't push past her comfort zone. She was absolutely certain of that. He may have tossed the first innuendo out there, but he'd waited for her reaction before continuing with the verbal foreplay. With every step deeper into intimacy, he assessed her reaction, and waited for her to accept his overtures.

She could get her feet wet in this new and exciting territory and give her confidence a boost without fearing she'd be dragged into a situation she wasn't ready for. The freedom to say what she wanted without worry was a heady rush.

"We should take this to your bedroom," he said, the hungry glitter from earlier exploding full force in his eyes. "That's where your shower is, right?"

Like he was actually thinking about the shower, rather than her bed.

"There's a guest shower right through that door." She nodded to the left.

She shuffled closer to him, so close she could feel the heat his big body shed, and the hot, musky scent of arousal surrounded her. Her fingers trembled slightly as they fumbled with his belt buckle.

The first time her fingers brushed his bare belly was unintentional. His muscles bunched at the accidental caress and a groan broke from him. He sounded as though he were in pain, except there were no bruises that low on his torso. She glanced at his face and caught an expression of such sensuality there was no doubt that what he was experiencing had nothing to do with his injuries, and everything to do with her touch.

Delighted with that discovery, she deliberately feathered the tips of her fingers across the hard plane of his belly as she slipped the strap out of the buckle and released the steel pin holding it in place. His big body quivered with each brush of her hand.

The fact that she could make such a gorgeous specimen of manhood quiver and quake with the mere brush of her fingertips may have gone to her head. Okay, it definitely went to her head. So did his hot, musky scent and the feel of his smooth, taut skin beneath her hands—so warm and tight and responsive.

She hadn't intended to continue the teasing past unbuckling his belt, but found herself caught in the web of sensuality right alongside him. Lord, if he felt this good right here, right now, with just the brush of bare skin on bare skin, what would it feel like to have him completely naked, on top of her? Inside her? She wanted to find out.

Continuing the slow, teasing glide of her fingers across his lower belly, she unbuttoned the top button of his jeans. He caught his breath and froze as she reached for the zipper.

The room was quiet, broken only by their increasingly thick breathing and the hum of the refrigerator in the kitchen. The silence seemed to cinch in around them, drawing them closer, amplifying the sensual heat and the building anticipation.

Until her doorbell pealed.

She jumped at the interruption, and the spell shattered.

"Son of a bitch." His voice was both guttural and clipped. "Ignore it."

She stepped back to give herself some breathing room, space that wasn't steeped in his scent and the heat from his big body. Slowly her head cleared.

"It's probably Kait," he said, swearing beneath his breath as the buzzer sounded again. "She's always had the most God-awful timing." He sounded disgusted.

She took a deep breath and some of the sexual urgency faded. "I won't tell her you're here, but I am not going to hide from her, either."

He scowled, but held his tongue as Demi headed for the door.

Before unlocking the deadbolt she checked the peep hole. A long thin face with a sandy thatch of sparse hair blinked back at her.

Slowly she pulled away. "Well, the good news is it isn't Kait."

"The bad news?" Aiden asked from directly behind her.

She started and spun around. Good God, the man moved like a cat.

"No bad news. It's just Chester. The guy you blocked from getting in the elevator."

An irritated look flickered across his face. "He can't take a hint?"

Demi snorted and shook her head with a tsk-tsk. "You mean telling him the elevator was occupied and shutting the door in his face? That's not a hint, that's bad manners." She turned back to the door and reached for the deadbolt. "Besides, he's probably just checking up on me, making sure I'm okay." She shot him a pointed glance from over her shoulder. "That's what good neighbors do."

Aiden muttered something behind her, but she couldn't make out what it was. Which was undoubtedly a good thing. It hadn't sounded complimentary.

"Chester," she said, smiling brightly as she opened the door. "What a nice surprise." Aiden muttered something beneath his breath again and Demi smiled even brighter. "You remember Aiden from the elevator."

Chester craned his neck to look over her shoulder and blinked a couple of times. His Adam's apple wobbled as he cleared his throat. "Sorry to interrupt, but I wanted to make sure you were all right. It looked like the elevator got stuck between floors for a while." His voice trailed off as he glared at the man behind her. "I called building maintenance. I'm sure they'll rectify the problem."

Unlikely, since the *problem* was standing directly behind her, bristling with impatience.

"That's so kind of you," Demi said, ignoring the derisive snort rising behind her. "And yes, that elevator incident was disconcerting."

Apparently, that was all the chit chat Aiden could tolerate, because he wrapped his arms around her waist from behind and deliberately drew her flush against his torso.

"As you can see, she's *fine*," Aiden said, his voice both flat and cold. "She's also busy, so you'll have to excuse us."

Before Demi could prevent him, he grabbed the edge of the door and swung it shut.

"Aiden!" Demi drove an elbow into his abdomen.

A choked groan sounded behind her and she had an instant of regret. She must have hit one of those ugly bruises. But then irritation swelled again—served him right. That uncalled for display of possessiveness was exactly why she needed to sit him down and have a talk with him before these fireworks zipping between them drove them into the bedroom.

"Okay, mister," she snapped, swinging around. She jabbed her forefinger into an unbruised spot on his chest for emphasis. "We need to have a talk before this goes any further."

CHAPTER SIX

We need to have a talk.

With Demi's threat ringing in his ears, Aiden took a cautious step back and regrouped. Any male past puberty knew that those were fighting words, the forerunner to an argument. The smart man tread carefully. Or evaded completely, if possible.

"All right," he said slowly, eying her scowling face warily. Time for evasive maneuvers. "Mind if I take a shower first? I could use a long hot soak."

"There will be no showering, at least not here, until we come to an understanding." She planted her hands on her hips and looked determined—a stance which might have carried more impact if she stood a foot taller and hadn't sported a head full of pink spikes.

Aiden grinned, even though it stung like hell.

She narrowed her eyes and glared at him. "You find something funny about that?"

"No, ma'am," he answered promptly. "You just look like a pixie standing there." Not that he knew what a pixie looked like, but when evasive maneuvers failed, the experienced operator stepped in with a distraction. He raised his gaze to her hair and assumed a considering expression. "Maybe it's because of all those pink spiky things in your hair."

Her eyes narrowed even further as she raked his frame from head to toe. "Considering the way you look right now, bringing appearances into it isn't helping your cause." She shot him a knowing look. "And in case you're wondering, Kait has grumbled—numerous times—about your propensity for winning arguments by using evasion and distraction. Guess what? I'm not falling for either."

Hell. Kait needed to learn to keep her mouth shut...

"We are going to talk, like a pair of adults, right here, right now," Demi said, her demand ringing out loud and clear in the enclosed space.

"Fine." With a bad tempered frown, Aiden raked a hand through his hair. "Look, I'll apologize to your friend, okay?"

Her hands dropped from her hips and a worried frown replaced the scowl on her face. "Good. You should. But that's not the problem. I'm thinking I may have given you the wrong impression."

He drew back and reassessed the direction the conversation was headed.

"I sincerely doubt it," he assured her.

She ignored the reassurance. "Obviously, there is a tremendous amount of chemistry between us." She waved her hand between them. "And if I'm not mistaken, you're as open to a ... physical relationship...between us as I am."

"You are definitely not mistaken," Aiden confirmed. Cocking his head and rocking back on his heels, he settled in to see where this odd argument was going.

"Great, but what you need to understand is that I'm not looking for anything permanent. What I want is a no strings attached, no emotions involved—friend with benefits." She paused and lifted her eyebrows meaningfully. "You know, sexual benefits."

Aiden barely caught his jaw from hitting the floor.

Was she serious?

He studied her face. She looked pretty damn sincere. Did she have no insight into her own emotional makeup?

"I'm not offering anything permanent," she stressed, apparently afraid he hadn't picked up on that little fact from her no strings attached, friends with benefits spiel moments ago.

"I'm not ready to settle down," she added.

Said the woman who had married her first love right out of high school and remained faithful to him through the seven years they were married, even though she'd been as insanely attracted to Aiden as he'd been to her—yeah, those signs had been impossible to miss.

Aiden swallowed a snort of pure disbelief. Lord help him, this was going to be as easy as shooting fish in a barrel. The woman had no idea that she'd just hog-tied herself. There was no way, absolutely no way, that Demi would be able to welcome a man into her bed and her body, with all the intimacy that entailed, and keep her heart hidden away.

The very act of lovemaking would tangle her emotions all up.

"Looks like we're on the same page, then," Aiden said, lying through his teeth. "I'm not looking for anything permanent either. No strings sounds like a winning proposition to me."

"*Really?*" She tilted her head and studied him. "I've been getting the distinct impression that you're looking for more."

"No kidding." He strove for a dumfounded expression. "Why's that?"

A conflicted frown feathered across her forehead. "Well, for one thing, there was that whole exchange with Chester a few minutes ago. Your reaction to his visit was far too possessive for a man who's looking for a fleeting, no strings attached fling."

He coughed and thought fast. To work his way into her heart, through her bed, he had to convince her he didn't have permanence in mind. And she was right, a man who didn't have any interest in permanence didn't get possessive over his lover of the moment. He needed a good excuse for his reaction to Chester.

"Hell." He ran a hand down his face and winged it. "You read that whole encounter with your neighbor wrong. I wasn't being possessive. At least not in the way you assumed."

"I did? You weren't?" She eyed him suspiciously. "Why don't you enlighten me, then? What was that about?"

"A guy like that...well, it's obvious he's pretty damn inexperienced," Aiden said, stumbling his way through the false explanation. "And he's fixated on you..." He checked her face to see if he was right. From the arrested look in her eyes, he was. "Odds are he asks you out constantly," he added, and knew he was on target from the unconscious little nod she gave. "And being the genuinely nice person you are, you let him down easy each time." He didn't have to check her face for cues on that guess, since it was a given. "So he clings to the hope someday you'll say yes and make all his dreams come true." He shot her a quick glance. So far it looked like she was buying this convoluted piece of fictionalized nonfiction. Now to tie it all together. "These are exactly the kind of guys who can turn dangerous if their fantasy is threatened."

"Chester? Dangerous?" She laughed in disbelief. "The guy's harmless."

He shrugged. "You don't know what kind of fantasies he's woven around you." She still didn't look like she was buying it, so he shifted gears. "Even if he doesn't turn stalker and try to force you to fulfill his fantasy, in the long run it's kinder to shatter any expectations a guy like that has, rather than lead him on—innocent as that may be." He raised his voice when she opened her mouth in clear protest. "Do you have any interest in going out with him?" Her mouth snapped shut. After a moment she reluctantly shook her head. "See, a guy like Chester—he's not going to move on unless it's made crystal clear he doesn't have a chance with you. Right now, and for the foreseeable future, he's so hung up on you he doesn't even notice any other girl that might be waiting for him." He paused long enough to assume a virtuous expression. "I was doing him a favor."

"Sure you were. You're a regular saint," she said dryly.

"I try." He pretended to preen, and knew he'd skated past that mishap by her snort of laughter.

"Okay, say I buy that load of crap you just tried to feed me." She gave him a dry, you-can't-fool-me- look. "What about what happened with Brett? You got into a fist fight with him simply because you thought he took me home. If you aren't looking for a serious relationship, why would it matter if he took me home or not?"

He studied her face. She hadn't believed a word he'd said about Chester, and there was no way he could spin what happened between him and Tag and make it believable. Time to stop spinning lies and give her the truth—with one crucial lie by omission.

"Fine, you want the truth?" He paused. Where to begin? Maybe at the beginning? "Do you remember when we first met?" He asked, watching her steadily.

"Sure." A look of reflection pushed the suspicion from her face. "It was a couple of weeks after I met Kait at that photography class. Donnie had gone to some kind of conference in Vegas. I was at loose ends, so Kait invited me to dinner. She cooked lasagna—some prized family recipe." She shot him a grin with a hint of nostalgia clinging to it. "You crashed the dinner party. Kait laughed, said she always made extra because it was your favorite dish and you always seemed to know when she was making it."

Another little perk of his gift. It was odd how the damn thing worked—how he could just suddenly know, with absolute certainty, that Kait was cooking the family specialty, or that a certain stock was going to hit the ceiling, or the long shot at the race track was going to surprise everyone and leave the rest of the track in the dust. And yet he'd not have a clue that the operator next to him, the teammate he'd gone through basic training and then BUDs with, the warrior who was as close to him as a brother—was seconds away from getting his head blown off thanks to a sniper's bullet.

At least Zane's—his CO's—premonitions were helpful. They saved lives.

What the fuck was his gift good for? Making money? Yeah, fuck that.

"You okay?"

Aiden shook his head to clear the frustration and get his mind back on business. They'd been talking about how they'd first met. The day that had irrevocably changed his life.

He caught her gaze. "You were wearing a yellow t-shirt with some kind of flower on it, faded jeans and sexy black half-boots with the longest damn heels."

Her hand absently went to her chest and her eyes softened. "It was an iris, the flower on the shirt."

He held her gaze steadily. "I took one look at you and wanted you. Right then. Right there and every day since."

Surprise flushed her face. "Really? I would never have guessed it. You never acted like it."

"You were married." He shrugged; enough said.

A small, tight silence hummed between them.

"I wanted you too," she admitted, without shame.

He gave her a gentle smile that barely hurt at all. "I know." The smile quickly faded and intensity took its place. "It's been ten years, sweetheart. Ten years of craving you, and locking the hunger down. And then Donnie died, and suddenly you were free...but drowning in grief and not ready for what I needed from you. So I waited...and waited, and waited some more for a sign that you were ready to take another man to your bed." He shook his head and grimaced. "This last rotation was pure hell. It was closing in on three years since Donnie died. I knew at some point those good old primitive urges were going to wake you up. When they did, I wanted to be the one you turned to."

"Oh... Her eyes rounded in understanding.

"Yeah." He rolled his shoulders and ran a hand over his head, choosing his next words with care. "So imagine my frustration to find that Tag had taken you home. Yeah, I admit I got a little possessive. But you were faithful to Donnie the entire time you were married to him. Let's just say I wasn't thrilled to find you were already involved in another relationship before I had a chance to work you out of my system." He paused and held her gaze steadily. "You have a history of faithfulness, sweetheart." Which he was counting on—his strategy for their future was dependent on that faithfulness. "How was I to know you were looking for a no strings fuck buddy?"

"You've wanted me for ten years? That's a long time to want someone on a purely physical basis, isn't it?" She was frowning again, the expression in her eyes conflicted—caught between suspicion and hope.

He shrugged. "Not really. It's a physical reaction. It's not like I'm obsessed with you." He fought like hell to keep his face straight. *Not obsessed with her? Sure—you keep telling yourself that buddy.* "And there were plenty of other women to distract me." Something flashed across her face, but he couldn't read the emotion. "Truth is, I haven't spent enough time around you to form an emotional attachment. I don't know much of anything about you."

Which was pure bullshit. While they hadn't spent significant time together, he knew enough about her. He knew the things that mattered. Like that she was loyal to a fault, had a wicked sense of humor, was completely open and unashamed of her sexuality, and was willing to compromise or even concede to those she loved. She'd confided in Kait she'd much rather live in a condo—because life was too short for lawn-mowing. Yet, Donnie had wanted the big old-fashioned house with the white picket fence and the huge front yard, so that's what they'd been saving for.

There was one other thing he knew, too. The most important thing. He knew, without a shadow of a doubt, that she wouldn't be able to keep her emotions under lock and key once they took that leap into the physical. It might take a while before she admitted it, but once they became lovers, she'd transfer her heart to him.

He was absolutely certain of that.

"Okay, so you aren't looking for a girlfriend. You're looking for a sex buddy," she said slowly, as though she were testing her conclusions in her mind even as she said them out loud.

"That's right." He held her eye, and tried to radiate sincerity.

And he wasn't even lying—at least not completely. He wasn't looking for a girlfriend. He wanted a hell of a lot more than that.

"Okay." She sounded a bit breathless. "Sounds like we're on the same page, then." She lifted her chin and gave him a stern look. "No more being rude to poor Chester, though."

He nodded in agreement. "As long as he doesn't turn psycho stalker. Terms are renegotiable at that point."

She rolled her eyes at that. "I told you, he's harmless." Her voice turned teasing, and her eyes started to sparkle. "So I guess the next step is for you to recover enough to get the job done."

Get the job done. He laughed as he stepped closer to her. The hallway was so narrow and confining; it trapped the rose scent that clung to her skin. Every movement they made stirred the perfume up, until it saturated the air. Something told him he was going to smell like roses from this day forward.

"You have such a romantic way of expressing yourself." He slung an arm around her shoulder and drew her to him. "Trust me. I'll have no trouble getting the job done."

"Big talk from a man who can't even kiss me." Her eyes laughed up at him.

His gaze narrowed. They'd see about that. Time to see if the ice pack had done its job.

He leaned in as she lifted her mouth to his, their lips touched and—"Sonofabitch."

Her laughter rang through the hall as he jolted back, his hand lifting to his burning mouth. Maybe he *should* visit Kait. She'd be able to reduce the swelling and ramp up the healing process. If he finessed the visit right, she'd never know he was camped out one floor down at Demi's place.

Piece of cake.

He just needed to slip away from Demi for an hour or so, and track Kait down.

CHAPTER SEVEN

Two hours later, Demi watched from the passenger seat of Aiden's Mustang as he pulled into the parking lot, and eased up next to her Volkswagen Beetle. Slowly, oh so slowly, he killed the engine to his vehicle, and set the parking brake—all without taking his eyes off her car.

Silence hummed between them.

"What happened to your Accord?" he finally asked, a grim tinge to the question.

What? He didn't appreciate her baby? "I traded it in. You don't like Maude?"

"Maude?" He shot her a suspicious look, as though he thought she was yanking his chain. "It's kinda pink, isn't it?"

Not kinda. Maude, her Volkswagen Beetle, was brilliantly pink. Iridescently pink. The kind of pink that could blind a person if they looked at it too long.

"Of course it's pink. It's a *ladybug*." She shoved open the passenger door and swung her feet over to the pavement before standing up.

"A *ladybug*," he repeated as he followed her out of the car.

"Of course it is. You should have painted it mauve. Then you'd have Maude the mauve ladybug."

She strangled a grin at that piece of whimsy. "But then it wouldn't match my hair. Besides, do you even know what color mauve is?"

"I know it's not pink." He turned to look at her over the roof of his Mustang, a hungry gleam glittering in his black eyes. Even with the lopsided swelling to his mouth and the ruddy knot along his cheek, he was strikingly, exotically, handsome. His gaze lifted to her hair and lingered. "You do like pink, don't you?"

"A lot better than mauve," she said, with a fond glance at her iridescent baby. She patted the roof as she hunted in her pocket for her car keys. "I'm going to paint a flirty set of eyes with twelve inch eyelashes across the backend."

"That will certainly up its resale value," he said, his voice totally devoid of humor.

Once again, Demi caught a grim, growly tone to his voice.

"What?" she demanded, turning from the car to face him. "She's pink. Big deal."

The freedom to do whatever she wanted to do, whether it was buy a bright pink Volkswagen Beetle or dye her hair a matching shade of fuchsia, was one of the benefits of being single. Donnie would have been mortified to be caught riding in such a colorful car. Nor would he have understood or accepted the artistic expression behind dying her hair such a flamboyant fluorescent shade. It looked like Aiden might be just as uncomfortable with outside-the-box life choices.

Well, so what? She wasn't married anymore. Nor was she going to curb her choices or style for a transient, fleeting fling. Even if the man was one of the most drool-worthy pieces of masculinity she'd ever encountered.

"My objection has nothing to do with the color," Aiden snapped, unleashing a scathing look on her baby. "That damn thing is so small a fender bender is gonna turn it into a tuna can. God help you if someone hits you going faster than thirty miles an hour. There's nothing there to protect you against a serious collision."

She could hear the concern beneath the growling and her chest warmed. It had been so long since anyone had worried over her safety, she'd forgotten what it felt like.

"It's safer than it looks," she assured him. "This model has a four out of five stars for front impact and a five out of five for side impact."

"From where?" he demanded, still scowling and not looking the least bit convinced.

"From Motor Trend," she said, smiling at him. "Trust me, I checked it out thoroughly before buying it."

He grunted, still assessing Maude, and Demi had no doubt that he'd be checking the safety ratings himself once he had access to a computer. That knowledge, had the strangest effect on her smile—increasing it by at least fifty percent.

Along the sidewalk that ran between the tavern's parking lot and the street, two college aged girls were chatting as they jogged. The girl on the right caught sight of Aiden and did a double take which sent her shoulder length brunette pony tail flying. She said something to her friend, who apparently had to look for herself.

Demi's smile fled as both skanks, in their way-too-short shorts that showed off their tanned, thighs and barely covered their asses, cut across the parking lot on a direct path toward Aiden. The blonde bimbo on the right actually had the gall to adjust her tank top for maximum boob spillage as she jogged toward them.

She vaguely heard Aiden say something, followed by the

scrape of his boots against the gravel as he turned to follow her gaze.

The girls dropped to a walk as they drew closer. Demi shot them her best back-off-he's-mine-glare, which they totally ignored.

Skanks...

Didn't they know the girl code? You didn't try to poach when the girlfriend was standing right there. Hell—for all they knew, he was married to her. They were too far away to see a ring, after all.

Of course...she glanced at the tavern behind her. It looked rather forlorn, squatting there with its windows shuttered and the fluorescent light overhead dead. Aiden was obviously dropping her off in front of her car, which was parked in front of a tavern. Even the least discerning person would assume they'd hooked up the night before. Maybe a pickup negated the code? Or maybe they were just a pair of skanks.

Yeah, she was going with skank.

"Excuse me," the blonde bimbo said, fluttering eyelashes so long they had to be fake, as she drank in Aiden's roughed up, good looking face. "We appear to be lost, would you happen to know—"

Aiden barely spared her a glance before interrupting, pure boredom in his voice. "I'm not from around here. Your best bet is to ask at the Subway up at the next intersection."

The blonde pulled back slightly, red flooding her cheeks, but she rallied quickly. While her brunette friend stood watching with wide eyes and building amusement, the blonde took another step forward. "I'm Barbie, and—"

Barbie? Seriously? She was Barbie? Of course she was.

Demi choked on a smirk, caught the wicked amusement in Aiden's eyes as he shot a glance at her and almost collapsed into a storm of laughter. She caught the impulse at the last minute and tried to smother it beneath a fit of coughing. From the rush of crimson to the Barbie doll's tight face, the girl wasn't fooled.

"Apologies." Aiden interrupted the blonde's dogged determination to make an impression on him. "But as you can see, my girl's unwell. We're pretty sure she's no longer contagious, but we won't know for sure until we get to quarantine."

Choking again, Demi helplessly released her keys to Aiden, who unlocked Maude's driver's door, opened it and practically shoved her inside. By the time she got her breath back the two women were clear on the other side of the street.

"Smooth," she said, wheezing. The smile from earlier bloomed again.

There was just something so sexy about a man who's eyes didn't stray after he'd committed himself to someone. But the thought stopped her cold. They weren't entering into a relationship that required a commitment. In fact, a commitment went against the no-strings deal they'd hammered out. So why the satisfaction that he'd showed no interest whatsoever in the banquet Barbie had so clearly offered him?

"I'm not the one who laughed in her face," Aiden reminded her dryly. He suddenly cocked his head and studied her. "What's wrong?"

"Nothing." Demi took a deep breath, suddenly off-balance and a bit dizzy.

Because of the laughter, of course. She'd lost her breath for a moment. That was all. There was no reason to feel like the earth had shifted beneath her feet.

"You okay to drive back home?" he asked, still studying her face.

"Yeah, I'm fine." She drew another deep breath and let it out slowly, relaxing as the dizziness faded.

"I'm going to swing by the house, pick up some things," he said, after a moment. "You going straight home?"

"No, I need to run to the store first." She decided, spur of the moment. "Then home." She leveled a sharp look at him. "No more fighting with Brett. Got it?" She wasn't sure she could survive a longer recovery period.

He raised his eyes to the sky in a long-suffering expression and shook his head. "Yes, ma'am." And then he braced his left arm along the top of Maude's door and leaned down, his big body blocking the sun. "By the way, I'll bring my own condoms to the party."

A shiver went through her. She wasn't sure whether it was because of his comment or because of his nearness. Probably both. Not that it mattered.

"But I bought so many...different colors...different textures....I thought we could have a fashion show." She batted her eyelashes at him.

Instantly an image of him strutting back and forth in front of her in nothing but a condom popped into her mind. Her skin flushed as heat flooded her—muscles liquefied, tingles swept her spine, butterflies tickled her belly. No doubt about it. He needed to heal *quickly!*

"Since we need to get out of here, I'm not going to ask what you're thinking," he told her in a sensual growl. But the gleam burning in his eyes told her he already knew.

He pressed in to steal a light kiss. The brush of his lips against hers was feather-soft and sweet and halleluiah, he didn't even flinch.

Pulling back, he straightened. "See you in a couple of hours?"

A couple of hours?

Disappointment crashed into her. She'd expected him to spend the afternoon with her, entertaining her with his banter, tempting her with his heat and hunger.

He pulled back, scanned her face and swore beneath his

breath. Leaning in he gave her another kiss, harder this time, with a hint of tongue. "I'm going to stop by and see Kait before I ring your bell, okay? Get some hands on healing. You're right. She'll do me more good than an ice pack."

The flip in her belly subsided. She pretended to preen. "You'll want to remember this moment and keep in mind that I'm always *right*..."

He straightened with a snort. "What you are is full of it. Which reminds me—you should eat something. Preferably something full of protein and carbs—for energy and stamina."

His tone was so level and his face so straight, she couldn't tell whether he was serious.

After another brush of their lips, he dragged himself away, returned to his Mustang, and roared out of the parking lot. Demi followed more slowly. The trip back to Coronado seemed to take an instant, thanks to her preoccupation. She stopped at the local supermarket and picked up several packages of meat— hamburgers, steaks, a roast. From comments Kait had dropped through the years it was clear Aiden was a carnivore. Then she spent far too long dithering in the beer isle. She knew he drank beer, but not which kind, and as a wine girl she had no clue what kind of brew he enjoyed. So she hung around just outside the isle and surreptitiously watched the men who entered it. None of them dithered, that was for sure. They zeroed in, grabbed and left. After watching several men choose the same brand, she grabbed a six pack herself and added it to the cart. Checkout seemed to take forever, not because the cashier was slow, but because Demi was impatient.

She meandered through town on her way back home, stopping to pick up fresh flowers and several bottles of wine. Aiden was welcome to his beer, but she'd stick to the good stuff. By the time she pulled into the complex's parking lot she'd managed to kill two hours. Aiden had said he'd head back to her place in *a couple* of hours. Exactly how many hours did that entail? Two, four? Five? She couldn't call him to ask, since she didn't have his cell number. Of course, he was at Kait's and she knew Kait's number, but Aiden had made it glaringly obvious he didn't want his sister to know about the arrangement between him and Demi—which she could understand.

Once the affair ended it would be awkward explaining the situation to Kait. It would be easier to keep her in the dark from the get-go. The last thing she wanted was her relationship with Aiden to affect her friendship with Kait. What if Kait thought Demi was using her brother, using him to scratch an itch only to discard him the moment the itch subsided...She frowned uneasily. Wasn't that exactly what she was doing? Of course, the scratching went both ways, but still...

She shrugged the uncomfortable feeling aside as she dragged the grocery sacks, wine bags, and flowers from the passenger seat. Aiden wanted the same thing she did...sex...sex... and more sex. It was nobody else's damned business what kind of an arrangement they'd agreed upon.

As she hauled the bags—which were getting heavier by the moment—into the lobby of her building, a tall, thin, frustratingly familiar man with a wispy shock of sandy hair exited the elevator. He caught sight of her and made a beeline in her direction.

Chester. Well...hell.

Too bad Aiden wasn't with her. He certainly had a way of driving off unwelcome admirers.

Regardless of her defense of Chester earlier, he often pressed past his welcome. Nor could she convince him that no meant no, or that she was uninterested, and would never go out with him. Maybe Aiden had been right. Maybe she *had* been too nice in her rejections. If she'd been harsher, and hadn't worried so much about hurting his feelings, maybe he'd have given up by now and moved on to someone new.

Maybe it was time to slip into her four-inch stilettos and give him a swift jab in the ass to get him moving along.

"Demi, my dear," he said stopping abruptly in front of her. "I am so happy to see you. We really need to talk. Here, let me help you with those."

How strange; his demand was eerily similar to the conversation she'd forced on Aiden earlier.

She sidestepped the hands reaching for the grocery sacks and hurried toward the open elevator. "I appreciate the offer, but I don't want to miss the elevator."

Ignoring her, he grabbed a bag in each hand. "Nonsense, there's no sense in you carrying all that weight when I'm right here to lend a hand."

Except that I don't want your help...

But as usual she swallowed her irritation. After a slight tug of war over possession of the grocery sacks, she gave in. Much more of this back and forth struggle and the bag's contents would end up all over the floor.

"Look, Chester," she said as soon as the elevator doors closed behind them. "Obviously I haven't been as adamant as I should have been." She glanced at his long, bird-like face and girded herself. Time to drive the point home. "So let me make this crystal clear. I'm not interested in going out with you. Not now. Not ever." She stiffened her shoulders as hurt filled his droopy brown eyes.

You're doing him a favor, Demi. Repeat after me: you're doing him a favor. He's far too fixated on you. Maybe this will sever those ties.

"I'm in a relationship with Aiden now, okay?" she continued. "You need to let go of this infatuation you have with me."

"This is exactly what we need to talk about," Chester said, his own shoulders stiffening. "He's not the right man for you. Surely you can see that? He's all wrong."

Seriously? He was telling her who was right for her. Did the guy have no social sense?

"Right." She snorted and rolled her eyes, relieved when the bell sounded and the light for the fifth floor lit up. "And I suppose you're the right man for me?"

It had been meant as a sarcastic retort, but she knew the moment his eyes lit up and he leaned forward, that the question had been a huge misstep.

"Yes. Exactly!" He reached for her hands, pure earnestness on his face.

As his hands caught hers, their grocery sacks collided. Wine bottles clinked.

"I swear to God, Chester, if you break any of my wine bottles I'm going to slap you up one side of this elevator and down the other." She'd seriously had it with the man. But as usual he totally ignored her.

"If you'd just give this emotion between us a chance, you'd see how perfect we are for each other. We were meant for each other, Demi. I intended to give you more time to recover from Donnie's death, but now that that horrible man is in the picture..." He gulped down a shallow breath. "No matter. You'll see that we're soulmates once we make love."

What the...had the damn man gone deaf and insane?

"There is no emotion between us, you dickhead," she snapped, marching out of the elevator the second the doors slid open. "Except for intense irritation. Give me my damn bags and stop bothering me."

She couldn't get any clearer than that.

When he didn't hand over the bags as requested, she stopped to glare. "I'm serious, Chester. Aiden's waiting for me in my condo. And he doesn't like you, so I'd take off while you can still see out of both eyes."

"He's at Ms. Winchester's," Chester said. "Which gives us

the perfect opportunity to explore these feelings between us without his interference."

Chester was spying on them?

A chill raced down her arms and legs. Aiden might not have been too far off in his earlier assessment of the man. For the first time in her three year association with Chester, a sense of foreboding struck.

This wasn't a case of a socially awkward misfit. Chester, obviously, had lost most of his marbles. It probably wasn't such a good idea to lead the man to her door. If he shoved her inside, and shut the door behind them...Aiden didn't have a key.

She was vaguely aware of Chester's voice yammering on in the distance as she tried to decide what to do, whether she should call out for a neighbor, or head to Kait's. And then suddenly his tall, thin body pressed into her, pushing her against the wall.

Her eyes widened as his head loomed closer. His mouth opened and fetid breath washed her face. She watched his eyes close, as his mouth headed toward hers.

Oh, hell no.

Without thought her knee rose—hard. There was plenty of room for it to build momentum as it headed toward his crotch. She jolted beneath the collision, but managed to hang onto her bags.

There was one short, intense moment of silence. The kind of silence that hung thick in the air after a major accident. And then he squealed like a greased piglet snatched from the mud, and dropped his bags—thank the good lord they were the ones without the wine. Crumpling into a moaning heap at her feet, he cradled his genitals.

"Hell," Aiden said from the open stairwell door to her right, the strangest mixture of amusement and satisfaction in his voice. "Remind me not to piss you off."

CHAPTER EIGHT

His heart still pounding from the breakneck race down the flight of stairs from his sister's floor, Aiden stepped into the hallway and let the stairwell door close behind him. For the first time ever, in the twenty odd years he'd dealt with the gift his Arapaho ancestors had unleashed on him, he'd known someone was in trouble.

It hadn't been a gradual dawning of knowledge either. Out of the blue, the absolute certainty had struck that Demi was in trouble. He didn't know how, he didn't know where, he just knew she was. He'd reacted on instinct. Escaping from Kait's apartment by rambling off some vague excuse he didn't even remember now, he'd let his body take over. It had driven him down the stairwell to the fifth floor—Demi's floor. He'd arrived just in time to watch that asshole from the elevator push her against the wall and try to kiss her.

"*Try*," being the operative word, since the attempt hadn't gotten ol' Chester far. Demi, bless her, had corrected the bastard's behavior with a forceful knee to the groin. She'd dropped the bastard on the spot, and from the squealing coming from the hunched over heap of clothing at her feet, the guy wasn't likely to present much of a threat anytime soon. Still, it never hurt to completely neutralize the enemy, regardless of how complacent they appeared, so he headed for the quivering mess on the floor.

He shot Demi a hard glance as he approached. "You okay?"

She gave him a jerky nod, briefly lifting her eyes to his. They were dark, slightly shocked, slightly outraged, and definitely filled with warning. "I don't need any I-told-you-sos."

Grinning, he stepped back, raising his hands—palms out—in the universal gesture for surrender. "Yes ma'am. No lip here. I like my family jewels where they are."

She smiled slightly at that and shook off whatever paralysis had her in its grip. Hefting her bags slightly, she stepped around Chester. "These bags are getting heavy. I'm going to drop these off at the apartment. I'll be back to collect the rest in a moment."

She meant the two her admirer had been carrying, and then dropped beneath the impact of her knee.

"I'll bring them in a second. After I've had a little chat with our friend." He waited, watching her carefully, but she didn't protest his intentions. Apparently Chester had used up all his good boy points with that asinine maneuver.

As she headed down the hall at a leisurely clip, the weight of the grocery bags dragging her shoulders down, Aiden squatted next to the man who'd tried to kiss her.

"You're lucky you're incapacitated," Aiden said in a casual voice. "Otherwise you'd be missing a couple of teeth, along with your balls." He paused, to let that threat sink in, but the asshole never lifted his head or gave any indication he even knew Aiden was there. "Since you're apparently unable or unwilling to take a hint, let me make this very clear. "If you pull this shit again, your balls will be the least of your worries. I'll rip your heart out and feed it to you one fucking slice at a time. You don't go near her, you got that? You don't think about her." The jackass still hadn't lifted his head, but he'd stopped rocking and moaning. "I'll be watching. You get within fifty feet of her and you're done."

With the warning delivered, Aiden collected the items sprawled across the carpet and returned them to the grocery bags. Rising to his feet he stared down at the thin figure curled on the ground. Most men would have shaken the pain off by now and headed for an ice pack and aspirin. This asshole looked like he had dropped anchor and intended to stay.

"You'd be wise to find a different place to live," he finally added, dispassionately.

With one last glance to assess whether the bastard was planning a sneak attack once Aiden's back was turned, he walked away. From the look of the guy, Demi's countermeasure had dislodged more than his balls, it had taken out his spine as well.

He reached Demi's apartment to find her door wide open. Shutting the door behind him, he continued into the kitchen and set his bags on the counter next to the ones she'd been carrying.

"There's beer in the car," she said abruptly.

She looked in one of the plastic bags and picked it up, carrying it to the fridge.

"Okay..." Aiden said slowly, watching her shove packages of meat into a compartment of the refrigerator.

Her body was stiff, tense—she wasn't nearly as blasé over what had happened in the hallway as she wanted him to think. When she closed the fridge door and headed back to the groceries, he moved to intercept her.

"Hey," he said softly, drawing her into his arms. For a moment it looked like she was going struggle against his hold, but then she wrapped her arms around his waist.

"I'm okay," she mumbled the words against his chest. A

huge sigh shook her and her body softened, melting in his embrace.

"I know you are." He kissed the top of her hair, and ran a soothing hand down her back. "But I've wanted to get my arms around you for a very long time."

He drew her closer. Christ—she felt good against him. Warm. Soft. Feminine. The scent of roses hung heavy around them. Did she taste like roses, too? Not that he knew what roses tasted like, but he sure wanted to find out.

"He just surprised me, that's all," she said, tilting her face up to his. "I guess you were right about him."

Yeah, and wasn't that a surprise considering he'd been talking out of his ass at the time. He froze for a second as it occurred to him that he could use this new development to his advantage.

"Between your knee and my chat, he's probably got the message. But I'll stick around for a couple of days to make sure he doesn't try anything stupid again." With a little finagling he could turn those couple days into a week and from there into a lifetime.

"Hmmm." A smile feathered across her face. "So trying to kiss me is stupid?"

"Only if it's unwelcome, and that knee of yours is cocked." He waggled his eyebrows at her, and glanced down at her leg. "So tell me, Ms. Barnes, is your weapon holstered?"

The smile spread to her eyes. "I'm beginning to think you're a tease. There you go again making promises—" She broke off, her gaze sharpening and zeroing in on his lip. "Holy shit, the swelling is almost gone." Her eyes narrowed thoughtfully as she reached out to stroke his mouth. "Kait?"

The caress was tender and sensual, and without pain. He caught her hand and kissed her fingers. No stinging, no burning. Just cool, silky skin beneath his mouth. Dropping her hand he raised his fingers to his lip and prodded the wound, still nothing. And Demi was right, the swelling was barely noticeable.

"I'll be damned. Apparently, cuts and bruises are easy for her to heal. It must take a hell of a lot more energy to knit bone and restore cartilage."

Or completely regenerate a spine.

She pulled back far enough to push up the t-shirt he'd pulled on back at his place. Tag and Trammel had been gone, thank Christ, so he'd managed to avoid the looming apologies. After packing a duffle bag in record time, he'd vamoosed. The apologies could wait. Getting Demi beneath him couldn't.

"The bruises are mostly gone too," Demi said, after a moment, wonder echoing in her voice. She ran her palms up his chest and then down his ribs. "Do they hurt?"

An electrical current zipped along the path of her hands, sparking a fire in his veins. His blood turned molten. His spine tingled. His scalp tightened. His dick sat up and howled.

"Something hurts, but it's not my chest." He caught her right hand and lowered it to just above his throbbing crotch.

Letting it go, he waited for her to make the choice on how far to take their sensual play. She seemed fine about what had happened in the hall. But the bastard had grabbed her and tried to force a kiss on her. Maybe she needed some time to recover. Maybe she wasn't ready for more than teasing.

"Hmmm." Her voice husky, she gradually, one tantalizing second at a time, slid her fingers down until she reached his crotch. As he helplessly arched into her hand, she cupped him and gently squeezed until a groan broke from him. "There's still considerable swelling down here."

"No shit, and it hurts like—" He lost his train of thought, along with his voice when she squeezed him again.

"Poor baby," she said between kisses as she brushed her

mouth along his chest to his right nipple, and paused for a quick suckle. "How 'bout I kiss it and make it all better?"

He was so focused on her hot, wet mouth and the effect it was having on his breathing—which was growing more strangled by the moment—he didn't notice the sneak attack on the zipper to his jeans until her hand stole inside his pants and underwear and hot fingers closed around his cock.

Jesus fucking Christ.

His eyes crossed and his heart tried to thump right out of his chest. Groaning, he thrust into her hand.

"The current swelling is quite...impressive," she murmured, her breathing audible as she stroked her palm down his penis from head to base. "But it appears to be growing even larger—which can't be good."

Grunting, he ground his cock into her hand again and groaned as she gave it a long, slow pump. "It's waiting for you to kiss it and make it better."

His voice was so thick and guttural he didn't think she understood him.

"You think?" Her voice was almost as thick and breathless as his.

Her mouth trailed kisses down his chest to his abdomen, where she stopped to nip and then lick. His belly twitched at the stinging caresses. Beneath the slow steady stroking of her hand and the stinging path of her mouth, it took him a second to realize she'd dropped to her knees in front of him. Each nip and swipe of her tongue was lower.

Son of a fuck...was she...

By the time her mouth reached the open zipper of his jeans his heart was pounding so hard he could hear it in his ears, and a ruddy haze veiled his vision.

She pushed his jeans and underwear down, a small hungry sound escaping her as his cock jutted straight up in the cage of her hand. He choked and held his breath as her mouth lowered.

The mind-blowing feel of soft, silky lips and the wet heat of her mouth closing over the head of his cock almost brought him to his knees. Except she pulled back and looked up at him.

She waited for his eyes to uncross and focus on her face, and then told him with absolute sincerity. "It doesn't seem to be working. The swelling's getting worse, not better."

"Wha...Wha..." He shook his head, trying to follow the curveball she'd thrown at him.

"I kissed it," she reminded him, her eyes so dark they were almost black and sparkling with heat and humor. "But it didn't make it better. In fact...from the amount of swelling going on... I'd say I made it much, much worse."

The little tease...

He bent down, rummaging in his jean's pockets until he snagged a condom and then dragged her up and into his arms. He pried off his right shoe with his left foot and vice versa, kicked off his jeans, and glanced around. The kitchen counter was too narrow for what he had in mind; the table, too round and fragile. He turned and headed for the living room.

"Whatcha doing?" she asked, her voice husky.

Rather than struggling in his hold, her arms twined around his neck and her legs around his hips.

"It's my turn to test this kissing hypothesis," he told her as he carried her through the living room.

Her head pulled back. Dark eyes laughed up at him. "It doesn't work when you kiss yourself."

He snorted out a laugh.

"Trust me." He nuzzled the side of her neck, then nipped. Turnabout was fair play after all. Smiling at the quiver that shook her, he stroked the sting away with his tongue. "I won't be kissing myself."

"But I'm not the one in pain," she reminded him, her fingers playing with the hair along his neck.

Hell, even that caress, slight as it was, tightened his scalp and sent chills crashing down his spine. It was time to get her as revved up as he was.

"That's because you have too many clothes on." Once he got her naked, he'd make her burn.

He walked through her bedroom door and glanced around, his gaze zeroing in on the bed. He'd showered in the guest bathroom, so he hadn't seen what she'd done with this room. But it didn't surprise him that a quilt covered her bed. Or that the quilt was pink—each square a varying shade, so together they made a pink rainbow of sorts.

Pink shadowed the walls too, although it was a more subtle, soothing color.

"You sure like pink," he observed, dropping her on the bed.

She squealed slightly in surprise as she bounced on the mattress, her eyes widening and promising retaliation. But they started to shimmer with heat as he pulled his t-shirt over his head. He bent to grab her ankles and dragged her to the edge of the bed. By the time he straightened after slipping off her shoes, she'd already removed her shirt and her fingers were on the front clasp of her bra.

"Let me," he said, his voice husky. "It'll be better than Christmas."

"Sounds like you've had some pretty shitty Christmases, then." While her laugh might have been light, the words wobbled slightly.

"I've just never been given anything so damn perfect before," he said in a rough voice.

The deep, thick pressure rising in his chest interfered with his speech, his breathing, and quite possibly his heart.

He dropped to his knees in front of her and set the condom

on the carpet, then reached for her bra. The clasp separated easily—thank Christ—and he pushed the straps down her bare, fragile shoulders until it slipped off her arms.

Jesus, she was absolutely gorgeous sitting there. Her hair tousled, the pink spikes matching the color blooming in her cheeks. Her breasts were small tight globes, the nipples peaked and rosy, a perfect fit for the palms of his hands. He cupped them, squeezing gently, and leaned forward to press a gentle kiss to the hollow of her throat. Slowly, oh so slowly, he trailed kisses down her chest to her right breast and took her nipple in his mouth. As he suckled one breast, he played with the other—squeezing the soft, round globe, pinching and releasing her nipple.

Her breathing grew rougher, her heartbeat erratic. His followed suit when one of her hands slipped between their bodies to cradle his balls. She mimicked his attention to her breasts, with her hand on his boys, until his cock throbbed like a son of a bitch.

Groaning, he pulled back. His hands shook as they dove for the button of her jeans, but by God he had them, along with her wet panties, off in record time. To her credit, she fell back and lifted her hips to help him along. Her legs were silky smooth and went on forever, but he was more interested in what was between them.

Draping her legs over his shoulders, he trailed kisses along the silky, soft skin of her inner thighs. The first nip sent a quake through her body, so he did it again, and soothed the slight red spot with more kisses. From the moan that whispered through the silent room, his kisses were having the same effect on her as hers had on him.

He wanted to grin, but the hunger was burning too strong, building too fast. From the tingle creeping along his spine, he wasn't going to be able to keep this up much longer. Abandoning the silky skin of her thighs for the even silkier moist flesh between her legs, he gently parted her sex and pressed a kiss against her wet opening.

Jesus, she tasted perfect. Sweet and salty against his tongue.

She jolted, a choked scream breaking from her.

Pressing closer, sucking on her, he felt her legs clamp around his neck, the muscles rigid and trembling. Her hips thrashed and a keening wail echoed through the room.

She was close, so damn close, just one more nudge...he thrust his tongue into her...once...twice.

Screaming, she went rigid against him, her legs so tight around his neck they came close to cutting off the oxygen to his brain. Ripples swept her, and then her thighs went slack. Unwinding her legs from around his neck, he grabbed the condom, ripped it open and rolled the rubber into place. His hands shook as he guided his penis into her.

He entered her with one hard thrust, pulled back, and thrust again, and then again. Her legs rose to curl around his waist as her hips rose to meet each thrust. He hammered into her repeatedly, straining above her, his gaze locked on the dark, liquid glaze of her eyes. The scent of roses swirled through his head. Her taste was still on his tongue, and the certainty that he had lost something and gained something and would never be the same rose within him.

And then she came again, the wet, tight flesh of her sex milking him, stroking him, driving him insane, and dragging him into the maelstrom—to shatter there inside her.

CHAPTER NINE

Demi returned to consciousness slowly, vaguely aware of a hot, damp weight pressing her into the mattress. Somewhere above her, someone groaned. A rough, deep, chesty kind of groan. A sound of utter exhaustion. The weight settled more heavily on top of her.

She thought about protesting, Aiden outweighed her two to one, after all, and the pressure against her chest did make breathing difficult. But it felt so good to have him there, on top of her, inside of her, driving her into the mattress. She'd been dreaming about this for months—hell, if she were honest, for years.

Sighing, she ran her hands down his back, reveling in the feel of sweaty, hard muscles beneath her palms. His body was such a textural delight—steel sheathed in satin. Hot satin...as though his big body held some internal forge that constantly radiated heat. He'd be all the blanket a woman would need on a cold, snowy day.

She smiled dreamily; they'd have to find some backwoods ski resort to test that hypothesis. Hole up in a cabin for some night time gymnastics after hitting the slopes all day. He skied, as did she; they could grab a weekend getaway sometime in the coming winter and—the daydream came to a screeching stop.

The winter?

Winter was a good six months off...in the future. This hookup had an expiration date; it wasn't supposed to have a future.

Unconsciously, her arms tightened around Aidan's waist. They'd agreed they were only scratching an itch, and once that itch was eased, they'd move on. She frowned, her palms slowly skating up and down Aiden's back. She didn't want to move on. Not yet, anyway. She was still itchy.

But then, they hadn't set an end date, had they? Why couldn't they continue seeing each other for a while longer? They were both single, unencumbered adults. There was no reason they couldn't continue this sex-buddy relationship as long as it worked for them both.

"What's wrong?" Aiden asked in a raspy, sleepy voice. He turned his head to press a kiss to the hollow between her shoulder and neck.

"I was just thinking." She tilted her head to give him better access and quivered as he nipped her neck lightly. She may have created a monster with all that nibbling she'd done on him before. But damn, he'd tasted good.

"Thinking's overrated," he told her huskily. He trailed kisses up to her ear and drew the lobe into his mouth to suckle it. His hand slipped between her thighs, stroking the sensitive, swollen folds protecting her sex. "It's best to feel..."

Oh yeah, she felt fantastic... Her legs fell open, silently encouraging deeper exploration. But those earlier worries continued buzzing through her mind, distracting her.

"So." She cleared a sudden rash of nerves from her throat. She might as well nail down a timeframe. That might silence the uncertainty. "How long are you expecting this thing to continue?"

He froze for a minute and then lifted his head, staring down at her with absolute stillness on his face and shutters in his eyes. "Why? You ready to move on?"

"God no!" Unbidden, the words burst from her, while absently her arms tightened around his waist as though to hold him in place.

Something flickered in his eyes, and his face softened.

She didn't want to scare him off by turning needy; guys hated that, so she smiled up at him and forced a flirty tone into her voice. "After the performance you gave, I thought I'd keep you around for a while." She paused, struggling to maintain the lightness. "I mean, if you want to stick around..."

It wasn't until the muscles of his back relaxed beneath her fingers that she realized how tense he'd become.

"Well, it would hardly be fair to split on you now," he drawled, his mouth dropping back to her neck. He pushed a finger inside of her and lightly scraped the wall of her sex. "We've barely gotten started."

Her hips arched beneath a rush of wet heat. Gasping, she pressed herself against his touch and struggled to draw breath. "We haven't?"

"Hell no." He scraped her clit with his thumb and slowly pumped a finger in and out of her.

Demi bit back a shriek, her muscles drawing tight around him, her arms turning into a vice and refusing to let him go. Dimly, she heard him laugh, a rough, velvety sound full of male satisfaction. That thick tension had seized her again, was cinching tighter and tighter with each stroke of his fingers and suckle of his lips against her neck, until it exploded, hurling her into the abyss.

This time, when she returned to awareness and opened her

eyes, she found Aiden staring down, watching her. She flushed, suddenly self-conscious. "What?"

Stroking the back of his knuckles down her cheek, he simply shook his head. "I've never seen anything more beautiful than you, when you come. You glow, and your eyes get so wide, bright, and liquid—" He broke off, flushing slightly. Apparently the self-consciousness was catching. Clearing his throat, he grinned. "You also come faster than any woman I've known."

Known? As in the biblical sense? The two interested Barbies from the parking lot flashed through her mind, and jealousy stung. How many women had he known? She barely snatched the question back before it hit the air.

None of your business, Demi. Besides, do you really want to know?

She forced her mind past that particular road block and tried to resume the teasing tone they'd fallen into throughout the day. "These past five hours have been non-stop foreplay. Let's just say the pump was primed."

"Or I'm damn good." To illustrate his point, his hand went to work between her legs again. Only this time he worked two fingers inside her.

She groaned, helplessly trembling beneath the dual caress of his thumb and fingers. Happy to give credit where it was due, she cleared her throat. "Let's call it fifty-fifty."

He chuckled, a dark chocolate rasp of a sound. "I don't think so."

Waves of tingling swept through her. Liquid fire pooled between her legs.

"You get so wet for me," he said.

Well, that would have been an embarrassing revelation if he hadn't sounded so full of wonder and satisfaction.

Kissing the side of her neck, he withdrew his hand and

lifted her hips slightly, groaning as her legs rose to wrap around his hips. And then he was inside of her—the hot, thick length of him filling her to the core. She arched into his thrusts, riding him as much as he was riding her, faster and faster, while the heat built and pressure increased and the only thing left in the world was the man locked in her arms.

When she roused after her third trip to the sun, he was sound asleep beside her. At some point he'd pulled out and collapsed alongside her on the bed, although a heavy arm was draped over her waist, holding her in place. Which was a damn good thing, since she was crowded along the very edge of the mattress, and in danger of tumbling off without the support of his arm.

She sighed, the contentment so thick it had weight and volume, filling her completely. Lifting herself, she braced her elbow on the mattress and her head in her hand and stared at him. He was so big, he took up most the bed, even though she had a queen sized mattress.

"I can feel you thinking," he said, his voice still rough around the edges, his eyes still closed.

A smile touched the corner of his mouth, which was—she peered intently—barely swollen at all anymore. Demi sighed, stroking a finger down his lips, grinning when he caught it gently with his teeth.

"We should send your sister a thank you gift," she announced, "After all, none of this"—her hand slid down to his penis and stroked it back to attention—"would be possible without her healing."

He grunted sleepily. She shifted her weight over her hip to ease the pressure on her elbow and almost fell off the bed. Would have fallen, if his arm hadn't tightened around her and dragged her on top of his big body.

"I think I need a bigger bed."

"Don't bother." He finally opened his eyes and pinned her with a glittering look. "You'll be under me most of the time."

She grinned down at him. "Or on top of you."

He slid his fingers through hair and leaned up to kiss her nose. "I'm always open to compromise."

That was good to hear. She hesitated, then shrugged. "I think that while we're..." She chose her words with care, not wanting to give him the wrong impression or scare him off. "Sleeping together, we should be exclusive to each other."

She drew a deep breath, ready to argue her case and explain why it didn't really change the nature of their earlier agreement.

"I can live with that," he said, with the strangest combination of satisfaction and amusement.

Frowning down at him, she studied his expression. The smugness was stamped across his face, too, like he'd just won some kind of battle or prize. She thought back, but couldn't see any reason for that complacency. Regardless, she needed to deflate some of that self-satisfaction, and she knew exactly how to do it. Straightening, she climbed off him and slid from the bed.

"Hey." He sat straight up in protest, pure sensual promise glittering in his heated gaze. "I wasn't finished with you yet. I'm about to prove once and for all that a real SEAL in your bed is a thousand times more satisfying than those books you and my sister devour by the sacksful."

She almost passed out from anticipation—but, first things first.

"I want to try an experiment," she announced, glee bubbling inside her.

His gaze narrowed, and he looked suspicious. At least for a second, before he noticed that she was naked. The suspicion shifted to hunger and his gaze dropped to her breasts. "What experiment?"

"Oh, it's just something I saw on the science channel the other night," she told him with an airy wave of her hand. "About how men react to the color red."

"So what's the experiment?" he asked, back to looking suspicious.

"I'm going to put on something red, and see how you react."

He swept her naked body with hot, hungry eyes. "Trust me, baby, nothing you wear is going to crank my engine like what you're wearing right now."

She grinned. They'd see about that. "Close your eyes. No peeking."

He groaned, but fell back on the mattress with his eyes closed. She collected the fuck-me-now ensemble from the night before and headed for the bathroom. It seemed to take forever to struggle into the outfit, and force her feet back into those punishing four-inch stilettos—which she thought was due to anticipation, at least until he shouted at her from the other side of the door.

"How much longer you gonna be, sweetheart? I've got some experiments of my own we can try."

She paused at the sultry promise in his voice before adjusting the neckline of her sweater for maximum boob spillage. "Almost done. Close your eyes." She listened to an onslaught of grumbling and choked back a laugh. "Are your eyes closed?"

"Yes." There was a definite bad tempered snap to his voice.

Apparently the man was used to instant obedience. She'd have to break him of that expectation. She opened the bathroom door and peeked around the edge to make sure his eyes were closed—then strode out in her, as Brett Taggert had put it, military grade weaponry.

"Okay, you can look." She posed at the foot of the bed with one hip jutted out for impact.

Sighing loudly, with a long-suffering expression on his face, he opened his eyes and lifted his head. His gaze locked on her face, before he did one of those up and down sweeps from the night before. For a split second his eyes widened in pure shock, and then a blast of arousal swept the room. He jackknifed up and off the bed.

"What the hell?" A thundercloud closed over his face. "You wore that to the Bottoms Up?" Horrified disbelief lifted his voice into a shout. "Are you crazy?"

Okay, that wasn't the reaction she'd been going for. Scowling, her hands dropped from her hips. "What's wrong? You don't like it?"

"Hell, yeah, I like it." He stalked toward her, his naked body powerfully beautiful in the filtered sunlight streaming through the skylights ringing her bedroom's A-framed ceiling. "As long as it's a private show, in a private place where the clothes can come off."

She stared at him, barely hearing the qualifications, mesmerized by the lean masculine grace of his stride and the play of muscles down his thick thighs and calves. To her disbelief, heat stirred again, a slow, languid slide through her belly and into her chest. The previous ravenous hunger had quieted, sated by their three—she did a double take as the number echoed through her mind.

Three times?

She counted off the sessions. Yep, three. Apparently the legendary stamina of SEAL team members wasn't an exaggeration.

He closed in on her, sweeping her up in his arms with no effort at all, and damned if that didn't get the tingles and butterflies going. There was something so sexy about a man in prime physical condition.

Her fuck me now attire came off a thousand times faster than it had gone on—exactly as intended. There was no doubt about it, those brain scientists were onto something, red really did get the male motor cranking—as Aiden called it. She needed to download the rest of the series and see what other interesting tidbits their documentaries had to offer.

She grinned at the thought. Now that would be an interesting way to keep the sparks alive.

Smiling, she reached up, welcoming him to round four.

You've just finished reading Hearts Under Fire, the first book in my Operation: Hot Spot series. You can find the rest of the books in the series here:

Trust Under Fire. Book #2. (Lucas and Emma)
My BookLoyalty Under Fire. Book #3. (Rio and Becca)

Future Under Fire, Book #4. (Tag and Sarah) This book will release mid-August. If you'd like to be notified when this book releases please add your name to this form.

https://forms.gle/NJfm5Yorpx7qQPdP7

Are you interested in new release news, and information on sales and contests? Then sign up for Trish McCallan's newsletter!

https://www.trishmccallan.com/newsletter-sign-up/

Keep reading for a preview of the second Operation: Hot Spot book, Trust Under Fire.

AUTHOR'S NOTE

If you enjoyed Hearts Under Fire, I'd appreciate it if you'd help other readers find this book by sharing the title and book description with your friends, reader's groups, book clubs, and online reading forums.

Additionally, leaving an honest review on Goodreads, Amazon or any other retail site would be appreciated. Reviews help cue readers into what they might like or dislike about a book. They also enhance book discovery.

As always, thank you for reading!

Your support is appreciated!

Find Me

Trish on Facebook: https://www.facebook.com/Trish-McCallan-Romantic-Thrillers-447327722108528/

Trish's Red-Hot Reviewers: https://www.facebook.com/groups/174504969903447/?source_id=447327722108528

. . .

Trish on Twitter: @TrishMcCallan https://twitter.com/
trishmccallan?lang=en

Sign up for Trish's newsletter: https://www.trishmccallan.com/
newsletter-sign-up/

You can find Trish's website at: https://www.
trishmccallan.com/

ABOUT THE AUTHOR

 Trish McCallan was born in Eugene, Oregon, and grew up in Washington State, where she began crafting stories at an early age. Her first books were illustrated in crayon, bound with red yarn, and sold for a nickel at her lemonade stand.

Trish grew up to earn a bachelor's degree in English literature with a concentration in creative writing from Western Washington University, taking jobs as a bookkeeper and human- resource specialist before finally quitting her day job to write full time.

Forged in Fire came about after a marathon reading session, and a bottle of Nyquil that sparked a vivid dream.

She lives today in eastern Washington.

An avid animal lover, she currently shares her home with three golden retrievers, a black lab mix and three cats.

SNEAK PEEK: TRUST UNDER FIRE

"What the hell?" a deep, frustratingly familiar voice thundered from somewhere above Emma. "Rio said you were getting a dog. What the hell is *that?*"

Emma froze and then slowly turned, finding Lucas Trammel, in all his six feet-three inches of overbearing glory barreling down the porch steps toward her in his customary worn jeans and t-shirt. His hair was wet, as though he'd just stepped out of the shower. She scowled as he headed toward her with that limber, far too sexy walk. The gait of a man in peak condition, in the prime of his life.

Her traitorous body went weak kneed and hungry. Her muscles heated, her skin tingled, her mouth watered. Sexual attraction revved her heart and respiration.

Not going to happen. Not ever again. Like ever.

"Lucas." She schooled her voice and face to ambivalence. No hurt. No anger. No embarrassment. Nothing to show how much he'd wounded her with his abrupt abandonment. "What are you doing here?"

His stride checked at her tone and the eyes locked on her face turned wary. "Rio called me." He stopped and cocked his head, apparently noticing her lack of familiarity with the name. "Dante Addario, the officer who responded to your 911 call? He's an old friend." He shrugged and ran a palm across the back of his thick neck. "He told me what happened."

Emma fought back a sour smile. Of course Officer Arctic was Lucas's buddy. She should have known from his surly disposition and lack of people skills.

"What do you want?" She let a hint of impatience creep into her tone. Better annoyance than hurt, or even worse—interest. He stepped back slightly, as though her attitude surprised him.

"I thought you could use some help," he said after a long pause.

"Thanks. I appreciate the offer, but I've got it handled." She forced a smile, but suspected from the sudden crinkle to his brow that she hadn't sounded all to sincere in her appreciation.

Another awkward pause, even longer this time, and the dark brown eyes watching her narrowed. "Rio's concerned whoever's responsible may return."

Concerned? Really? Officer Arctic? She swallowed a derisive snort.

"If they do, I'm prepared for them," she told him with all the confidence she could muster. "I've taken steps to protect myself."

Her eyes were desperate to soak in that long, lean body she remembered so well, far too well after thirteen weeks of abstinence, so she locked her gaze on his jaw. That chiseled chin, with its hint of a dimple, was about as safe as it got when it came to the man in front of her.

"Steps?" he repeated, his gaze dropping to the dog sitting patiently at her side. "Is that one of your *steps*? When Rio told you to get a dog, he meant an actual dog, not an oversized rat."

Emma bristled. Nobody made fun of her Cuddles. *Nobody.*

Before she had a chance to force feed that disparaging description down his arrogant throat, the animal he'd maligned exploded into another of those deep, vicious, Rottweileresque growls.

Lucas did a double take, his eyes widening.

Ridiculously pleased with Cuddles's response, Emma bent over to give her an appreciative petting. "Good girl. You showed him who's boss."

"Right," Lucas drawled, with a shake to his head. He stepped back and appeared to reassess. "I just meant that when it comes to dogs and protection, the bigger the better." He glanced down at Cuddles who was still snarling at him and his eyebrows climbed so high they merged with his damp, mocha colored hair. "And it sure as hell helps if they have some *teeth*."

"Cuddles will do just fine," she said stoutly. Setting her jaw, she narrowed her eyes and glared, daring him to argue. "She'll bark and alert me to strangers on the property, which will give me a chance to protect myself."

...hopefully...

"Cuddles?" He snorted and rubbed the back of his neck again. "Yeah, that name just inspires fear."

"Look, go away, alright? I don't need your help." The request came out much sharper than she'd intended. Something he'd obviously picked up on since that earlier wariness returned to his square face.

Ambivalence, Emma. No hurt. No anger. No embarrassment. No emotion.

He said something softly beneath his breath. Although she hadn't heard it clearly, she was pretty sure it was a swear word. With a frown, he ran a tense hand through his hair leaving it tousled and sexy and unbearably reminiscent of those nights in his bed. Unwelcome memories flashed through her mind.

Burnished shoulders arched above her...his hard, tight face dripping sweat...the sleek skin and rippling muscles of his back beneath her hands...

Whoa! She pulled back hard from the memory, praying it hadn't blazoned itself across her face. She was over him damnit —she was!

"Look..." An awkward, uncomfortable look dug into his face. "I should have called you back sooner. I'm sorry, okay? I was out of town and—"

"Sooner?" she interrupted in pure disbelief. "*Sooner?*" Her voice climbed. "This unwelcome visit does not count as a call back!"

And there went her mask of ambivalence.

"Emma—" Gentleness touched her name. Regret flashed across his face.

She flinched. "Don't. Just don't." She took a deep breath, and regrouped. "How long have you been back in town?"

He scowled, and rolled his corded shoulders. She could see the play of muscles through his gray *American Sniper* t-shirt. "I don't see—"

"*How. Long?*" she snapped.

He studied her face and swore beneath his breath again. Yep—definitely a curse word.

"Two months, give or take."

Two months? The breath huffed out of her. "See? We have nothing to talk about."

He squared his shoulders and set his jaw. "Regardless of how things ended between us, I still consider you a friend."

A friend? Really? *Really. He's playing the we can still be friends card?* And here she hadn't thought things could get more humiliating.

"And friends help friends," he continued doggedly.

Was the man insane?

Buy Trust Under Fire Here